MY BOOK

THEO Waits

GREAT STORIES
ABOUT HORSES

GREAT STORIES
ABOUT HORSES

COMPILED BY ELEANOR M. EDWARDS

ILLUSTRATED BY HAMILTON GREENE

Hart Publishing Company

NEW YORK CITY

ACKNOWLEDGEMENTS

Grateful acknowledgement is made to the copyright owners for permission to reprint the following stories:

A GROWN-UP COULD HARDLY HAVE STOOD IT abridged from *The Autobiography of Lincoln Steffens,* copyright, 1931 by Harcourt, Brace & World, Inc; renewed © 1959, by Peter Steffens.

THE PRINCE'S FOAL from *Wonder Tales of Horses and Heroes* by Frances Carpenter. Copyright 1952, by Frances Carpenter. Reprinted by permission of Doubleday & Company, Inc.

THE KIND CALIPH AND THE HORSE THIEF from *Wonder Tales of Horses and Heroes* by Frances Carpenter. Copyright 1952 by Frances Carpenter. Reprinted by permission of Doubleday & Company, Inc.

A HORSE AFRAID OF HIS SHADOW from *Wonder Tales of Horses and Heroes* by Frances Carpenter. Copyright 1952 by Frances Carpenter. Reprinted by permission of Doubleday & Company, Inc.

JEB STUART, BOY IN THE SADDLE by Gertrude Hecker Winders, copyright © 1959 by the Bobbs-Merrill Co., Inc.

THE ROYAL GREENS by Russell Gordon Carter, copyright 1940 by Story Parade, Inc.

CAN A HORSE KNOW TOO MUCH? by Genevieve Torrey Eames, copyright 1945 by Story Parade, Inc.

SUCH A KIND WORLD from *Nellie and the Orphans,* by Mabel Leigh Hunt, copyright 1946 by Story Parade, Inc.

IF WISHES WERE HORSES by Adele De Leeuw, copyright by the author.

NO SUM TOO SMALL by Murray Hoyt, copyright 1947 by Murray Hoyt.

WASHINGTON'S SCOUT copyrighted 1951, by F. A. Owen Publishing Company; publisher of The Instructor.

CONTENTS

List of Illustrations

The Royal Greens

RUSSELL GORDON CARTER

ON A COOL misty autumn morning in the year 1777, as David Wethervale led the small black mare from the stable, his father said to him, "After today I reckon you'll have to go to school afoot."

David's hand tightened on the bridle, and he swallowed hard. He said, "Then—you have at last found a buyer for her?"

"Aye," Seth Wethervale replied. "A man from over Danbury way is coming tomorrow. I'm sorry, lad, for your sake."

David made no comment, knowing the futility of further pleas and arguments. His father had made up

9

his mind to sell the mare almost a year earlier, soon after Uncle Charles had died from wounds at the hands of Johnson's Tories in York State, leaving the horse to his brother-in-law. At that time Seth Wethervale had said, "She's too light for farm work. I'll have to sell her."

As David rode slowly westward toward the schoolhouse at the Corners, some three miles distant, he was miserable. No one knew the full depths of his feelings for the little mare that had enabled his uncle to carry dispatches for Washington's army. "Hobgoblin," she was named, because of her swift ambling gait and her curious facial markings—a generous spattering of little white flecks that gave her a strange and frightening look. Yet, in spite of name and appearance, she was one of the gentlest horses in western Connecticut. And now, after almost a year of wonderful comradeship, he was about to lose her! It made David feel completely miserable.

Halfway to school, as they were crossing the old wooden bridge over the swift waters of Dog Creek, one of the rotten planks gave way under Hobgoblin's weight, and she stumbled and pitched her rider sidewise into the stream. David scrambled out, breathless and shaken, his hose and breeches dripping. Hobgoblin gazed at him wonderingly, then began to nuzzle at his shoulder. Her manner seemed regretful and apologetic.

David threw an arm impulsively over her drooping

neck. " 'Twasn't your fault," he said. " 'Twas that rotten plank. Lucky you didn't break a leg!"

He removed his shoes and proceeded as best he could to squeeze the water out of his clammy breeches. Half an hour passed before he mounted again.

School was in session when David tethered the mare in a pine grove across the road. As he entered the small square building, Mr. Verrill, the schoolmaster, frowned and tightened his thin lips.

"What made you late?" he demanded. "Did you dawdle?"

"No, sir, I pitched off my horse," David replied. "She went through a plank in the bridge, and I landed in the water."

Several of the smaller girls tittered.

Mr. Verrill glowered at them, and the sound subsided at once. "Take your seat," he said to the boy.

After David had sat down between Mary Jacobus and Joseph Trumbull, the schoolmaster reopened the brown-covered speller on his desk and proceeded to call upon the pupils at the front of the room. But David's mind was not on the lesson. He was thinking of Hobgoblin, wondering miserably what would become of her. Would the man from over Danbury way treat her kindly? Would he put her to heavy work?

"David! Stand up and spell 'independent.' "

Joseph Trumbull's elbow against his ribs roused David to the realization that the schoolmaster had

Hobgoblin...stumbled and pitched her rider
sidewise into the stream.

called on him. He got slowly to his feet. What was the word Mr. Verrill had asked him to spell? He heard Mary Jacobus whisper something.

"Indignant," he began. "I-n-"

"The word was 'independent!' " Mr. Verrill broke in sharply.

David's thoughts cleared. "Oh, yes, sir. Independent. I-n-d-e-p-e-n-d-a-n-t."

"Wrong!" cried the master. "Who can spell it correctly?"

The schoolroom buzzed with eager voices.

"Now try it again, David."

The boy wrinkled his forehead. Even amid the buzz of eager voices his thoughts had again strayed to the mare. He began uncertainly. "I-n-d-i-g"

Mr. Verrill sprang from his chair, his face flushed. Seizing his birchwood ruler, he motioned with it to a corner. "Stand over yonder with your face to the wall!" he ordered. "Maybe 'twill help you gather your wits."

David was ashamed of himself. Yet even now, as the lesson resumed, he was unable to give his full attention to it. As he shifted uncomfortably from one foot to the other, his thoughts were once more for Hobgoblin. If only there were something he could do to make his father change his mind.

Half an hour dragged past. With head against the wall, David was listening to Mary Jacobus trying to spell "beatific," when she suddenly uttered a startled

exclamation and then began to laugh. Glancing sidewise, he saw a surprising sight. Through the open window close to Mary protruded Hobgoblin's white-
flecked head, her ears twitching, her jaws gently chewing a wisp of grass that hung from her lips. Others
began to laugh, but a sharp crack of the ruler on the
desk brought sudden silence in the schoolroom.

"David!"

"Yes, sir?"

"Why did you not tie up your horse?"

"I—I did, sir."

"It does not look so!"

"She must have freed herself, sir."

"Well, go and tie her up again! You and your horse
are a vexation!"

*Through the open window close to Mary protruded
Hobgoblin's white-flecked head . . .*

David hurried outside. He thought he had tied the bridle rein securely enough to a young pine, but here it was hanging free. Gathering it up, he led the horse away from the schoolhouse — not back to the pine grove, however, but up the hill to where a solitary apple tree stood above grass that was still long and green.

"There now," he said as he secured the rein to a limb. "You can graze here all you please."

He lingered, caressing Hobgoblin's smooth neck and letting her nibble playfully at his shoulder. Must he leave her and return to the schoolroom? With a renewed sense of misery, he allowed his gaze to wander far off. To the east he could see the clustered houses of the village and, to the north of it, the round powder-house built of field stones. Close by stood Amos Thatcher's big barn, which now held all the supplies for the militia. His own house lay out of sight in a valley beyond the town. His gaze lowered to the road winding among patches of woodland, dropping to Dog Creek, then gradually twisting upward toward the Corners.

Suddenly he stiffened and caught his breath. There on the road a quarter of a mile from the Corners a body of men was marching—men with muskets, upwards of two score of them and all clad in dusty green uniforms! He stared, almost unable to believe his eyes. Men in green uniforms marching toward the town!

His throat went abruptly dry as the explanation leaped to his mind. Tories! A detachment of the Royal Greens, Johnson's Tories, who had fatally wounded his uncle a year earlier! They must have come up the old logging road that joined the main road some two hundred yards below the Corners. Now they were doubtless on their way to destroy the militia supplies while the men-folks were at work in the fields!

David jerked the bridle free from round the limb. A moment later his leg was across the gray blanket that served as saddle, and he was on his way down the slope, circling toward the west in order not to be seen from the road.

Mr. Verrill, ruler in hand, was at the door when the boy reached the schoolhouse.

"What is the meaning of this?" he demanded. "I told you—"

"There's a party of Royal Greens down yonder on the road!" David interrupted him breathlessly. "They aim to raid the town—"

"Eh, what? I say—here, now! David, where ye goin'—" The schoolmaster's voice trailed off into a blur of sound as horse and rider went quartering down across the field.

Reaching the main road, David drew rein and held Hobgoblin to a slow walk. He knew exactly what he would do. Just beyond Dog Creek a second logging road joined the main road from the north. He would

There on the road . . . a body of men was marching . . .

follow the raiding party at a safe distance until he was across the bridge, then he would strike up the logging road till he came to open country and then rush eastward as fast as possible. He was sure he could reach the town in time to give the alarm.

David was riding now through an old beech wood, the mare's hoofs making hardly a sound on the soft earth at the right of the road. Ahead of him he could hear Dog Creek tumbling over its stony bed as it raced southward to join a branch of the Housatonic. The sound grew louder as he approached the base of the valley. Overhead a pair of crows called raucously.

Just ahead of him the road turned to the right before it dropped steeply to the creek. David drew rein and listened, but heard nothing except the roaring of the creek and the calling of the crows. Probably the raiders were by now already across the bridge. He urged the horse round the turn and then jerked her to a sudden halt, his heart almost in his throat. Less than fifty yards in front, on the near side of the bridge, marched the raiders!

For an instant David sat rigid, viewing the collapse of his careful plan. He could never reach the north logging road now, and if he were to turn back, the surprise of the town would be complete. The thought was intolerable! Acting on swift impulse, he clapped both heels to the mare's flanks, and away she went straight down the incline.

The suddenness of his charge took the Tories unawares. He saw green-clad figures drawing hurriedly
apart in front of him. The wind sang in his ears. The
woods rang with the clatter of hoofs and the shouts of
men as Hobgoblin thundered downward, her haunches
straining, her mane flying, sparks leaping outward
from beneath her pounding feet. Something slashed
at him as he bent low over her neck. A musket butt
glanced off his shoulder. Another swished through the
air and struck the mare's haunch, causing her to leap
sidewise. A branch raked his face as he swung her back
in the middle of the road again.

Only one man was between him and the bridge! He
saw the fellow raise his musket threateningly, but
before he could fire, Hobgoblin struck him with her
shoulder, sending him spinning. The bridge now was
only a score of yards distant and seemed to David to
be rushing at him at breakneck speed. In a terrified
instant he pictured what would happen if one of Hobgoblin's feet should go through the hole. Then he
steeled himself. He had taught her to jump. She must
jump now—for her life! Almost at the edge of the
bridge he tightened his legs under her and let his
weight fall backward. "Now, girl, now!"

Hobgoblin responded beautifully, landing almost in
the center of the bridge. Then she was thundering up
the slope beyond. Two or three musket shots rang out
as she reached the first turn, and he heard the bullets

snap overhead. A moment later horse and rider were round the turn—safe!

But there was no time to waste. David dug his heels against the mare's flanks, urged her to her utmost. When they reached the first house on the outskirts of the town, she was wet and glistening.

A woman appeared in the doorway, wide-eyed.

"Tories!" David shouted, slowing down. "A big band of them on the road!"

Through the heart of the town he clattered, shouting the warning on all sides: "Tories! Two score of the Royal Greens!" Then he made off across the fields where he saw men working.

"Tories!" he shouted. "They're on their way up the west road!"

Somewhere in the town a bugle blared, the uncertain notes quivering across the countryside. On a rise of ground David brought the mare to a halt. He had done his best. From all directions, from the woods to the north and the fields to the east and south and west, men in shirt sleeves were running toward the town— sun-browned, resolute men with scythes or axes in their hands. He saw the first arrivals enter Amos Thatcher's barn, saw them emerge with muskets and powder horns. Others joined them, and as they formed ranks, he caught sight of his father.

It was only when David saw the hastily formed column moving off down the road to the west that he realized the full significance of what was happening. There would be a battle. Men would die, his father, perhaps. He felt suddenly faint. Slipping from Hobgoblin's back, he led her to a gulley and sat down heavily on a rock.

How long he sat there he never was able to determine. From the west came the sound of firing, first a volley, then a second volley, then scattered shots at long intervals, then silence. The faint odor of burnt powder presently touched his nostrils. He stood up, then sat down again. He was cold, too cold to sit still.

He rose to his feet once more and, clutching Hobgoblin's bridle, made his way slowly to the town.

Women and young children gathered bewilderingly about him, and he tried as best he could to answer their excited questions. Finally one of the women said, "Let him be now. He's overwrought. Sit ye down here on the step, David, whilst I go and warm some milk for ye."

It was not until well past noon that the militiamen began to return. David saw them come straggling up the hill, and in one group, to his profound relief, he spied his father.

Seth Wethervale came forward at a quick walk. His face was powder-stained.

David ran to meet him. "The Tories—" he began.

"They're in York State by now, them as is left," his father replied grimly. Then his rough hand reached

The suddenness of his charge took the Tories unawares.

forth and clutched his son's shoulder.

"Lad, I be proud o' ye!" he said. "What ye done an' all—"

David smiled and shook his head. " 'Twas Hobgoblin," he protested.

Seth Wethervale nodded. "I know all about it! Mr. Verrill told how you rode headlong down the road right through the midst o' them—"

" 'Twas Hobgoblin," David repeated.

For a long moment father and son looked full at each other—a moment vibrant with understanding.

Finally Seth Wethervale said, "I reckon ye're right. The mare shares the credit." Then he added in a tone meant to be matter-of-fact, "And I reckon, after what's happened, 'twould be a mite unfair to part the two o'ye."

David felt the warm blood come flooding into his face. "You—you mean you'll not sell her after all?"

"Aye, lad, that is what I mean. You've earned the keep of her."

David stared with eyes bright and lips parted, too deeply moved to speak. With a boisterous shout, he suddenly whirled and ran to where Hobgoblin was patiently waiting. A moment later his arm was across her neck and her soft lips were against his shoulder as he told her the joyous news.

A Horse Afraid of His Shadow

FRANCES CARPENTER

ONE DAY, long, long ago, in the ancient Eastern land of Macedonia, the horse market in its capital, Pella, was crowded with buyers. King Philip II, himself, was there. With him were the keepers of his royal stables. A fine lot of horses had been gathered for selling. First choice would go to the King and his warriors.

At the side of King Philip stood his young son, Alexander, a boy then twelve years of age. None in that throng of buyers had a better eye for a good horse than this lad. No boys of his own age in all Macedonia could compare with the young Alexander in horsemanship.

"Look well at all the animals, my son," King Philip said. "Then tell me which ones you would choose from among them."

"Many of these colts are well formed, my father." The boy spoke with sure tones. "Many have spirit. They would ride bravely to battle. But none is so noble as that young black stallion yonder, that one with the white mark shaped like an ox's head on his face."

"The young Prince chooses well," the black stallion's owner cried. "That is indeed the finest colt in all the market today. My price for him is high, thirteen talents, in fact. But I will be honest with you, Your Majesty. That young black stallion will wear a saddle and bridle, but he will not be ridden. He is wild as the North Wind. None can stay long upon his back." The black colt even then was prancing and snorting as the noisy crowd gathered round him.

"No other horse here can compare with that one," the boy, Alexander, insisted. "Surely skilled horsemen from the palace stables can tame him."

"Let the black stallion be ridden!" King Philip gave orders.

The most daring horsemen of his court mounted the colt. But the trader had spoken truly. One after another, they were thrown from his back when they attempted to ride him over the plain.

The colt started at every sound. As soon as one tried to ride him away, he whirled and reared high. He gave one mighty twist, and his rider was gone from his back.

"Are you satisfied now, my son, that this horse is not worth the buying?" the King asked Alexander.

"No, Father, I still say the black stallion is the very best in this market place. His riders do not understand him. Let me try my hand on his bridle."

The King was pleased with his son's courage.

"Ride him, then, Alexander!" the King said. "And if you can succeed where these others have failed, I will buy the horse for you."

The men in the horse market marveled to see the fearless lad leap into the saddle. The trembling black horse stood still. The boy stroked his glossy neck, which shone like ebony. Alexander talked to the horse softly. Then he turned his head straight toward the afternoon sun and galloped away over the plain.

It grew late. The sun was dropping below the horizon when the anxious crowd in that market place saw the boy coming back. Like lightning, the black stallion was galloping, galloping, but the boy was still on his back. Easily Alexander pulled the spirited steed to a halt. He patted the sides of the stallion, which now seemed tame as a kitten.

"Well ridden, my son! The black stallion is yours," King Philip cried.

"Tell us your secret, young Prince," the palace horsemen asked. "How did you tame that wild spitfire so easily?"

"It was as I said," Alexander replied. "You did not understand him. This stallion is a horse of high and noble spirit. He starts at the sight of each moving thing that is strange to him. While the others were trying to ride him, I saw that what frightened him the most was his own moving shadow. When he ran from the sun, the black shadow leaped along, just under his nose. I took care to turn his face toward the sun, so that his shadow could not be seen. The horse forgot his fear. I let him gallop to his heart's content, and now he trusts me as his master."

The King wept for pride and joy in his son's wis-

dom and bravery. "One day you will make a great king, Alexander," he said to the Prince. "But you must seek larger kingdoms. The one I shall leave for you will be too small for your powers."

Bucephalus, the ancient Macedonian word for "ox-head," was the name Alexander gave this favorite horse. The shining black stallion with the ox-head blaze on his face carried the Prince through many a battle. So tame was Bucephalus that he would kneel down, like a camel, for his young master to mount. Yet, throughout his life, this spirited horse would carry no other rider.

Then he turned his head straight toward the afternoon sun and galloped away over the plain.

When he was twenty years old, the young Prince succeeded his father on the Macedonian throne. Many were the countries conquered by this Alexander, whom men called The Great. To Greece and to Egypt, to Persia, even to India, he led his Macedonian warriors. As his father foretold, he did indeed seek and conquer broader kingdoms. So great were his deeds that people began to believe Alexander must be descended from the gods themselves.

Now, in that part of the Eastern world, there was also a kingdom known as Phrygia. When the Phrygian King died, the people had begged the gods to guide them in choosing their new ruler.

"Who shall next be our King?" they asked the gods. The answer, which they called an oracle, came through the priests in the temple. "Your King shall come riding to you in a wagon," the oracle said.

Hardly had the priest given the message of the gods, when Gordius, a wise but poor country fellow, rode into the public square in his farm wagon. At once the people cried out, "The oracle is fulfilled! Gordius shall be our King!"

In thanks to the gods, Gordius set his farm wagon up in their temple. He tied it in place with thick leather thongs. And he made the knot so skillfully that none could untie it.

People called this the Gordian knot. A legend grew up about it. This foretold that the man who could part its tight thongs would one day become ruler of all the world.

Princes of many lands, and other young heroes tried to undo the Gordian knot. But it was not until Alexander the Great came on his black stallion, Bucephalus, that the deed was done.

At first Alexander also tried to untie the Gordian knot. His fingers, too, failed to pull its thongs apart. Then, losing patience, but determined to succeed, the King drew his sword. With one swift thrust he cut the knot and the leather thongs fell apart.

Cutting the Gordian knot was an example of Alexander's way of taking a short cut to success. That is why when someone solves a difficult problem with daring and skill, we still say today, "He cut the Gordian knot."

Bucephalus was Alexander's faithful companion in battle throughout his life. The noble stallion lived to be thirty years old, a good age for a horse.

One story tells how, at last, in a battle in India, the brave horse, Bucephalus, was sorely wounded. Straightway he galloped out of the fray. He carried his master to a safe place before he fell to the ground. On that spot by the Indian river, Hydaspes, Alexander the Great founded a city. In loving remembrance of his favorite horse, the Emperor of the Eastern World gave the city the name of Bucephala.

Jeb Stuart, Boy in the Saddle

GERTRUDE HECKER WINDERS

IT WAS A CHILLY NIGHT early in January. Jemmy was studying his Latin lesson by the open fire in the living room. He had missed his lessons that day because he had gone hunting. His brothers were away at a private school.

He looked up from his book. "Mother, when am I going to have a horse of my own?" he asked.

His mother sat at her desk writing in a big account book. She frowned. "I don't know, Jemmy. We can't afford it now."

"But I need a horse, Mother. Father is away on Firebrand most of the time. The boys took their horses

back to school with them. All I have to ride is a plow-
horse or a mule. I can't ride in a fox hunt with either
of those! Last week I had to ride a mule down to the
west field to hunt. I'd have been ashamed if anybody
had seen me."

"Never be ashamed of being poor, Jemmy. Our
family is rich in honors." She nodded toward the picture over the mantel. It was a portrait of Jemmy's
great-grandfather, Major Alexander Stuart. He was
wearing an officer's blue coat trimmed with gold braid.
A small sword hanging under the picture flashed in
the firelight.

"Your great-grandfather fought in our War for In-
dependence," Mrs. Stuart said. "He was a very brave
man. Even the enemy admired his bravery."

"I know, Mother," said Jemmy. He had been told
a great deal about the Stuarts and the Letchers. The
Letchers were his mother's relatives. "I know your
Grandfather Letcher was a famous judge. I know
Father was an officer in the War of 1812. But what
has that to do with my not having a horse?"

"Just this. Our families served their state instead of
making money. They helped to make our country what
it is, but they didn't grow rich. We just don't have the
money to buy another horse now, Jemmy. You mustn't
feel ashamed to ride a mule if you have to."

The Stuarts were not really poor. They lived in a
big house set among great oak trees on a hill. The gar-

dens were filled with beautiful flowers. The paths were lined with hedges.

Jemmy's brothers went to a private school. Later Jemmy would go away to school, too. There were no public schools nearby. The Stuarts agreed that their boys must be educated as gentlemen should be.

However, the farm was not large. Mrs. Stuart ran it with only a few field hands. They raised small crops of corn, tobacco and sweet potatoes. All sorts of vegetables grew in the kitchen garden. There were chickens and pigs as well as cattle.

Furthermore, the woods were full of game and the streams of fish. The long dining room table at Laurel Hill was always filled with good things to eat. Company was always welcome, but the Stuarts didn't have much money.

Tobacco was the only crop they sold. They could have raised larger crops if they had wanted to. Mr. Stuart and the boys could have worked in the fields. But gentlemen didn't do work like that in Virginia in the year 1842.

Jemmy turned back to his book. "I'd rather have a horse than anything in the world," he sighed. He was nodding over his book when his father appeared in the door. Mr. Stuart was splashed with mud from riding boots to hair. His face was pale.

"Archibald!" exclaimed Mrs. Stuart, dropping her pen. "What is the matter?"

"Archibald!" exclaimed Mrs. Stuart, dropping her pen.
"What is the matter?"

Jemmy ran to his father. He put his hand on his father's arm. "Did Firebrand throw you?" he asked anxiously.

"No, Jemmy, but I have bad news. Elizabeth, I did a foolish thing, I'm afraid. I bought a horse, a fine little bay that——"

Jemmy's heart beat fast. "How could that be bad news?" he asked himself.

"Oh Arch, you didn't!" cried Mrs. Stuart. "You know we can't afford another horse."

"I—I traded tobacco for him."

"That is bad news," said Mrs. Stuart. "We don't need the horse, and tobacco is as good as cash."

"My dear, you haven't heard the bad news yet. The horse was a bargain. I could have traded him for double what I paid, but——" He sank into an armchair and dropped his face into his hands.

Jemmy put his arm around his father's neck. He looked from his father to his mother with worried eyes. "Was there an accident, Father?"

"Yes, Jemmy. The horse jumped away from something in the road as I was leading him home. A sharp rock sticks out from a bluff on one side of the road there. The horse fell on the rock and cut his leg. He's ruined, Pete says. There's no hope. We must kill him."

"Oh, no!" Jemmy and his mother cried.

"Can't someone cure him?" asked Jemmy.

"If the leg isn't——" Mrs. Stuart began.

"Pete says there is no use calling anyone. He says nobody can help."

"Why? Is the cut too deep to heal?" Mrs. Stuart wanted to know.

"No, Elizabeth. The cut could heal all right. But the horse is upset and refuses to eat or drink. He will starve to death. I've seen such cases before. I'm afraid we'll have to shoot him."

Tears rose in Mrs. Stuart's eyes. Jemmy blinked back tears himself. "May I see the horse, Father?"

"It will break your heart, Jemmy. He's a beautiful little bay——" Mr. Stuart choked.

"Surely something can be done," said Mrs. Stuart.

"If you'd see the horse, you'd understand. He's trembling and plunging in his stall."

She shivered. "I don't want to see him."

"I do," said Jemmy.

With his father he went out to the stable. Pete held a lantern high so that Jemmy could see the horse. The horse was trembling all over. His eyes were rolling

"Good boy," said Jemmy softly.

The horse tossed back his head and showed his teeth. Jemmy drew back.

"Don't try to touch him," said Mr. Stuart. "He's naturally a nervous animal. The pain has made him almost wild. Be careful."

"I can't stand to have him killed," Jemmy declared. "I just can't! Look at his neck, Father. He's more beau-

tiful than Firebrand!" He went on softly and coax-
ingly, "Why can't you be good? You're going to be
all right."

The animal turned his head toward Jemmy.

"He likes that, I do believe," said Jemmy's father.

Jemmy carefully put out his hand and patted the
horse. He didn't tremble quite so hard. Jemmy kept
on talking and petting.

"Pete, bring a bucket of water," ordered Mr. Stuart.
His voice shook. "Maybe Jemmy can coax him to
drink some water."

Pete brought the water. As soon as Jemmy held up the bucket, the horse jerked back his head. He kicked with his sore leg.

"No use," said Mr. Stuart sadly.

Pete nodded. "I've seen horses like this before. They won't let you do a thing for them."

"We'll wait until morning," said Mr. Stuart, with a thoughtful frown.

Jemmy hung his head as he followed his father into the house. If he hadn't been nearly ten years old, he would have cried like a baby.

Pete held a lantern high so that Jemmy could see the horse.

Usually he went to sleep the moment his head hit the pillow. Tonight he tossed and twisted. He just couldn't sleep. The wind whistled around the house. It rattled the windows, but it was not the wind that kept him awake. He was thinking of the beautiful little horse.

Finally he jumped out of bed. He pulled on his clothes and slipped downstairs. Then he ran through the darkness toward the stable.

"Did you think I'd forgotten you?" he began softly as he stepped inside the stable.

Firebrand made a noise. Jemmy spoke to him as he passed his stall, but he didn't stop. Firebrand didn't need any help.

The new horse was stamping and kicking. Jemmy touched him and felt him quiver. As Jemmy kept on patting him and talking to him, however, the horse became quiet.

"I wonder what I should call you," said Jemmy. "Father said only that you are a bay. He means that you're reddish-brown in color. Many words rhyme with bay—hay, way, say, may—I believe I'll make up a little poem about you.

> "I want my bay
> To do my way,
> He must eat his hay
> And here I'll stay!"

He piled straw on the floor and lay down. He went to sleep immediately. Presently the horse moved and wakened him. Again Jemmy quieted the animal. He took another nap. Again he was awakened.

"I thought you were settled for the rest of the night," Jemmy said. "You're as uncertain as—as a candle in the wind. That gives me an idea. I'll call you Bayberry."

Friends in Norfolk had sent the Stuarts some candles made of wax from bayberries. The candles had a pleasant odor when they burned.

"Bayberry," Jemmy repeated. "I like that."

For most of the night Jemmy soothed the horse. When light shone through the door, he said, "I'm thirsty and you'd better be."

At the pump by the horse trough in the yard he filled a bucket. He had to use both hands to hold the bucket up to Bayberry.

"Drink, now. I know you want a drink," he said softly. "Come on, you silly horse. Drink."

Bayberry dipped his nose in the water. Then he lifted his head and looked straight at Jimmy. "Drink. A real drink. Please," begged Jemmy.

Bayberry lowered his head and gulped a good, big drink.

Jemmy's knees shook. He sat down on the stable floor with the empty bucket beside him. That was where he was when Pete came in.

"He drank, Pete! He drank! Now I know I can get him to eat, too."

Pete's eyes opened wide. His jaw dropped. Then he dashed off to tell Mr. Stuart.

Being Practical

For the next week Jemmy spent most of his time in the stable. His lessons were forgotten, but nobody seemed to care.

Every night he lay on the straw beside Bayberry's stall. He slept in short naps. At the first sound, he was on his feet, ready to soothe Bayberry.

The very first day Bayberry had behaved well. He was quiet. He ate and drank.

Happily, Jemmy asked his father and mother to come to the stable to see him.

"You do have a way with horses," his father said. "I feel hopeful about him now."

"We don't need to worry any more about that horse," his mother said. "The idea of killing him! What were you and Pete thinking of?"

Bayberry began to tremble. He snorted and tossed his head. He kicked and Jemmy saw blood coming from his wound. Jemmy's heart sank.

"Oh, I spoke too soon," said Mrs. Stuart. "Why, the horse looks wild! Be careful Jemmy. He's dangerous. I know he is."

A tight lump swelled in Jemmy's throat. Had all his work been for nothing? Was Pete right?

He felt his father's hand on his shoulder. "Don't be disappointed if you fail, son. We hope you can save him, but we won't be surprised if you don't. There's not much chance."

Bayberry grew quiet after his visitors left. He was usually quiet when Jemmy talked to him. When Jemmy stopped, he began to shake. Sometimes he would eat his oats as he should, but not always. Jemmy didn't know whether he was going to cure Bayberry or not. Certainly he couldn't go on talking to him forever, as he was doing now.

One evening Jemmy went to the house to wash and change his clothes. His mother made him eat supper at the table with the rest of the family.

"Bayberry ate tonight," Jemmy announced. "Pete says——"

At that moment Mandy brought in another plate of hot biscuits. "Pete says that new horse is about to kick down the stall," she said.

Jemmy threw down his napkin and rushed out to the stable. He didn't sleep much that night. But the next day Bayberry was better, and the next day better still.

A week later Jemmy proudly led Bayberry out to the watering trough. The horse still limped, but not badly. For the first time Jemmy got a good look at him. His coat was red-brown, but his legs were black. He was beautiful.

In another week Bayberry was entirely well.

"Come to the porch after breakfast," Jemmy said one morning. "I'll show you a fine horse."

He sat proudly in the saddle as he rode Bayberry around from the stable. Pete followed. He was shaking his head and saying, "I can't believe it."

Jemmy's father, mother and three big sisters came out on the porch. The day was cold. They could see snow on the Blue Ridge Mountains in the west. A north wind rustled the dry vines on the porch pillars. Little Colly pressed her nose against the glass of a front window. She had a cold and could not come out.

"I can't believe it, either," his father said.

"Oh, I want to ride him," Bethenia said.

"We've never had a bay with black legs before," said Ann. "Isn't he a beauty?"

Colly beat on the window. She was saying something that nobody could hear.

"What's she saying?" asked her father.

"They all listened. Even Jemmy on his horse could hear her this time. "Is this Jemmy's horse?" Colly yelled at the top of her voice.

Jemmy's heart leaped. With shining eyes he looked

at his mother.

"Jemmy saved us a great loss," she said slowly. "But the girls need new dresses for the ball in Taylorsville next month."

Jemmy's heart sank. He knew each dress took fifteen yards of silk, and silk was expensive.

His father was frowning.

"I'm sorry," his mother added, "but we must be practical. We need the money. I think we should sell the horse at once."

Jemmy bit his lips as he leaned over to pat Bayberry on the neck.

"A bay with black points," Jemmy thought. "I've never seen one before." His eyes sparkled. "That's the only kind of horse I'll ever want to own now."

"He is a beauty," said Ann. "Look at him arch his neck. Do I dare pet him?" She put out her hand to stroke his nose, but Bayberry tossed his head and reared.

"I was expecting that," Jemmy laughed. He sat easily in the saddle as he soothed Bayberry. "He's pretty skittish, but I like a horse with plenty of spirit."

"I won't ask if I can ride him," said Bethenia. "He's too lively for me."

"And for me," echoed Mary.

"The horse will bring a better price if he's trained," said Mr. Stuart. "This accident may have frightened him. Jemmy should ride him for a while before we try to sell him. He should make sure the horse can still jump fences."

"Hurrah!" yelled Jemmy. He wheeled Bayberry toward a low place in the hedge. He loosened the reins and clapped his knees tighter on the horse. Under him

he felt Bayberry rise easily. Jumping the hedge was like flying.

His sisters clapped their hands. He looked back to wave as he galloped off.

"How straight he sits in the saddle," said Ann.

"He took the hedge beautifully," said his father.

He sat proudly in the saddle as he rode Bayberry around from the stable.

"Jemmy seems to be a part of the horse when he rides," said Mary proudly.

"I wish he could have a horse of his own," Bethenia said.

"So do I," said his mother slowly. "Jemmy's a born horseman."

The only thing Jemmy could hear as he galloped away was his mother's voice. "We must be practical," it said. "We must be practical."

The Highwayman

Jemmy never had liked to go to bed. He had spent many nights on straw in the stable, however. Now he was glad to be in his own featherbed. "I'm glad I don't have to wake up until morning," he thought a few nights later. He pulled the blanket up closer around his neck.

He had slept only a little while when he was wakened by a hand on his shoulder. "Wake up!" He heard Ann's voice. She sounded frightened.

"Bayberry!" said Jemmy, sitting up.

"Colly's sick," Ann exclaimed. "Nothing that Mother or Sally or Mandy can do for her is helping at all. We must have Dr. Melton."

Jemmy's bare feet hit the cold floor. "I'll go get him at once."

"Wait, Jemmy. I know you could, but I'll have to talk to Mother. She's afraid to have you ride so far alone at night. But there's nobody else to go. Pete and the other hands say they'd lose their way."

Jemmy's father was in Taylorsville that night. He was to join a fox hunt in the morning.

Jemmy picked up his shirt. "I'll go across the fields. It's only about four miles that way. Tell Mother I can ride Bayberry with my eyes shut."

"Of course you can, but she keeps saying, 'Jemmy is only a child. What can we do?'"

Ann hurried from the room. Jemmy called after her, "Remind her I'll be ten years old!"

He hurried into his clothes, fastening buttons with both hands. When he went downstairs, Ann was poking up the fire in the living room. She was wearing a white night cap and a long blue robe. Jemmy saw a rifle lying on the desk.

Ann picked it up and put it in his hands. "Take this with you," she said breathlessly. "You may need it. You know Father always carries a pistol at night. Mother knows you won't get lost. She's worried about a highwayman."

Ann nodded. "Shelby Carter was robbed the other night near the big oak tree."

"Why, I didn't know that!"

"Father told Mother, but he said not to tell the rest of us. He didn't want us to worry about him when he was on the road. That's why she's afraid to have you go out alone now."

From upstairs Mrs. Stuart called, "Ann, Ann!"

"Coming," Ann answered. At the door she looked back. "So take your gun!" she said.

Jemmy frowned at the long gun in his hand. "This is a clumsy thing for a fight on horseback," he thought. "Why, it's nearly as tall as I am. I wish I had a pistol."

In the fireplace a flame leaped high. Light danced on the sword hanging over the fireplace. Jemmy's heart beat faster as he looked at the sword. Of course! He took the sword and its scabbard down from their resting place.

In the stable yard Pete had Bayberry saddled and ready to go.

"Take care of this rifle for me," Jemmy said. He gave Pete the gun. "Now help me tie this sword to the saddle."

As he trotted down the lane, he drew the sword from its scabbard. He could reach it easily with his right hand. "I can use this if I have to," he thought. He slid it back into the scabbard and rode on through the darkness.

It was very dark. Wind sent black clouds racing across the stars and the moon. It twisted the bushes

He took the sword and its scabbard down from their resting place.

and trees along the road and blew cold on Jemmy's face.

Jemmy looked sharply to right and left. Familiar things looked strange in the darkness. There was a big oak tree two miles down the road. He would cross the fields there. Before reaching the oak, the road went up a steep hill and then down.

"I can't see a thing except the white bark of the sycamore trees," he thought. "I'll just have to feel when I've gone two miles. The road is level near the oak and that will help."

He passed the hill and the road leveled out. He spurred Bayberry on. "I wish we could run," he said to himself. "If only the moon would shine!"

At that moment the clouds began to part. Presently the moon shone like a round silver tray. Jemmy could see wheel marks in the road. Not far ahead he could see the oak tree.

Suddenly Bayberry snorted, and Jemmy's heart missed a beat. At the left of the road a man was crouching under the big tree.

Jemmy's heart rose in his throat. He began to tremble. Then he grabbed his sword and shouted at the top of his lungs. He spurred Bayberry forward at a gallop. He swung the sword above his head and yelled loudly.

The man jumped up. Jemmy saw that he had a dark cloth tied across the lower part of his face. The man stood still for a moment as if he didn't know what to do. Then he dived into the bushes and disappeared.

Jemmy turned Bayberry off the road and started across the field to the right. He felt warm all over with excitement. He slipped the sword back into its scabbard.

"I'm glad I brought the sword," he said to himself. He grinned and sat a little straighter in the saddle. He felt ready for a dozen highwaymen.

He hurried on as fast as Bayberry could go. In some places the ground was softer, and the horse struggled through mud. Jemmy could feel it splashing against his cheeks.

More clouds crossed the sky, hiding the moon. The night was darker than ever now, and Jemmy had to guess his way. He peered ahead into the darkness. He slowed Bayberry to a walk. If he didn't see a house soon, he knew that he had come too far to the right.

Bayberry waded across a narrow brook. On the far side the land rose in a low hill. On top of the hill was a dark shadow, a clump of trees. Jemmy was growing worried now. Surely he had come far enough. He urged Bayberry on.

When he reached the top of the hill, he could see the trees more clearly. Beyond them he could see something else, something dim and white. Then the moon peeped out, and Jemmy saw the tall white house of Dr. Melton.

The trip seemed shorter when Jemmy rode back

with the doctor. They met nobody.

Dr. Melton chuckled when Jemmy told him about the highwayman. "I'll bet it was your shout and not your sword that scared him," Dr. Melton said. "You boys can yell like Indians."

Back home, as Jemmy was putting the sword in its place over the fireplace, Ann and Mary came into the room.

He swung the sword above his head and yelled loudly.

"Oh, Jemmy, Dr. Melton says that Colly will be all right," said Ann.

"I know," Jemmy nodded. "Mandy told me."

"But the doctor got here just in time," Mary added. "She might have died if——"

She stopped and her eyes grew wide as she stared at the sword. "What are you doing with that?" she asked. "You won't believe me," Jemmy said. He told them about the highwayman.

"Jemmy!" Ann gasped.

"Weren't you scared?" Mary asked.

"Well, yes," Jemmy admitted. "But I didn't really have much time to be scared!"

Jeb Is a Good Name

It was the morning of February 6, 1843. "What a way to celebrate my tenth birthday," Jemmy thought as he jumped out of bed.

Yesterday a man had come to look at Bayberry. "I want a horse for my wife," he said. ' It must be gentle." Jemmy had hoped that Bayberry would act up. Instead he had been as gentle as a lamb. The man had offered a good price for him.

"Mother said she must talk it over with Father," Jemmy thought. "Why didn't she say that Bayberry wasn't for sale? Will she let me keep him, after all?"

After bringing the doctor home, he had hoped his mother would see that they needed Bayberry.

"Hurry, Jemmy," Colly called up the stairs. "There are birthday presents for you."

Only ten days ago Colly had been very sick. Now she was dancing up and down in the hall below. So was Victoria.

Jemmy put one leg over the stair rail and took make-believe reins in his hands. "Here I come on my horse," he cried. He slid down, face forward. At the bottom he leaped over the stair post.

Colly and Victoria laughed with delight. Then Colly gave him a piece of white paper. A smaller piece of black paper was pasted on it. "It's from Vickie and me," she said. "We made it for you ourselves."

"It's beautiful," said Jemmy, smoothing it out. "Thank you very much."

"I printed my name on the back," said Colly.

Jemmy turned the paper over. There in big capital letters was Colly's real name, Columbia Lafayette Stuart.

"It's such a long hard name, too," said Jemmy. "I'm glad you put it on the picture. Then I won't forget who made it."

"I pasted," said Victoria. She put a fat finger on the black patch.

"Do you know what it is?" asked Colly.

"It's a fine picture," Jemmy answered.

Colly waved her hands. "Tell what it is."

Jemmy hesitated. He didn't want to hurt his sisters. But he didn't know what the black spot was supposed to be. Just then Ann came down the stairs. Jemmy looked at her anxiously. She moved her lips to form the word *Bayberry*.

"Bayberry!" Jemmy exclaimed. Now he could see that the odd shape did have a tail.

"He could tell!" Colly shouted. "He could tell it was Bayberry!" She skipped to the dining room, and the others followed her.

Jemmy's favorite breakfast was waiting for them on the long dining room table. There were fried chicken, ham and grits and gravy. There were hot biscuits, peach preserves and apple butter, too. Beside Jemmy's plate was a pile of presents his sisters had made for him.

Ann had made him a pincushion with red roses on it. Bethenia had painted a picture of a horse in water colors. It was a strange-looking animal, with a big head shaped like a bucket.

Mary had a sampler for him. She had sewed his initials, J. E. B., on a square piece of cloth. Beside them she had put the date of his birth, February 6, 1833.

"Why, your initials spell a name, don't they?" Ann said. "Jeb."

"Mother, why do I have three names? All the rest of you have only two," Jemmy said.

"We named you for Judge James Ewell Brown of Wythe County," said his mother. "We liked the sound of the three names."

"I like the sound of the three initials better," Jemmy said. "Jeb is a good name."

His father handed him a small box. "Your brothers sent you this," he said.

Jemmy's hands trembled a little as he lifted the lid of the box. He couldn't imagine what it contained. Inside he found a pair of silver spurs.

Jemmy couldn't speak. Beautiful silver spurs, and he had no horse! He looked at Bethenia's picture of Bayberry. Then he looked at Colly's poor little cut-out. If only Bayberry were his!

"Did you really know my cut-out was Bayberry?" Colly wanted to know.

"I knew it was a horse right away," Jemmy said. "I had to look at it for a minute to be sure it was Bayberry himself, though."

Everybody laughed, but Jemmy didn't feel like laughing. Everything reminded him that Bayberry might be sold.

His father nodded toward the window and smiled. "Here comes Bayberry himself," he said.

Jemmy sprang to the window. His heart was pounding. Pete was leading Bayberry across the yard, toward the house.

"I'm giving you a new saddle for the horse," Mr. Stuart said.

Jemmy caught his breath and looked at his mother. She nodded. "Bayberry is yours. I don't know what we'd have done without him the other night. We'll just have to afford him."

Jemmy's shout was almost as loud as his yell at the highwayman. He rushed outdoors and threw himself into the new saddle. Then he galloped off for a ride over the farm.

The Kind Caliph
and The Horse Thief

FRANCES CARPENTER

IN BYGONE TIMES, certain parts of East Asia were
governed by rulers called caliphs and judges called
cadis. In those lands then, as in lands today, there were
good rulers and bad rulers. There were good judges
and bad judges.

Some of the caliphs thought only of their own
pleasures. "Let the poor people do as best they can,"
these selfish caliphs said. "It is not our affair if some
are homeless and hungry, or if some are wrongly
judged."

But in those times, as today, there were also good
rulers. There were good caliphs who looked well after

their people. There were good cadis who made sure bad men were punished and good men were rewarded.

A good ruler, indeed, was one Ben-Assar, whom all called the "Kind Caliph." Ben-Assar cared a great deal whether his people were fed and well housed and justly treated. Often and often, he put on the dress of a common man, and went forth to find out for himself how his people fared. Many a cadi's court did he visit to see whether his laws were being obeyed.

Well, one day this Kind Caliph chose to hide himself under the robe of a merchant. So clad, he called for his horse, and so, unknown, he rode through the countryside.

Ben-Assar had not gone very far from his capital city when he was hailed from the roadside. A whining man limped to the side of his horse.

"Good sir," he cried, "I pray you, give me a ride upon your fine horse. See how lame I am! See how slowly I travel on my old wooden crutch!"

Ben-Assar's good heart was touched by the sight of the cripple. "Whither do you go, my friend?" he asked the poor, limping fellow.

"Only to the market fair in the next town, kind sir," said the lame man.

"Well, I suppose there is room for the two of us on my horse," the Kind Caliph said. "Get up here behind me. I should be hardhearted indeed if I refused to give help to a cripple like you." So, both on the horse's

"Good sir," he cried, *"I pray you, give me a ride upon your fine horse."*

back, they rode slowly into the next town.

"Here is your fair, my friend," the Kind Caliph said, pulling his horse to a stop on the edge of the market place. "Get down now, and Allah go with you. Do not bother to thank me."

To the Caliph's surprise, the man did not move. No thanks were forthcoming. Instead, the lame man rudely cried, "Get down yourself, Merchant!" The Kind Caliph was almost speechless in his amazement.

"And why should I get down?" he demanded at last.

"So that I may ride along home on my horse," the bold cripple replied.

"But this is *my* horse," the Caliph cried. People from the market stalls gathered to listen to the dispute.

"Ah, no, it is *my* horse," said the rogue. "Nearby is the house of the Cadi, the wise judge of this town. We can let him decide which of us is the horse's master."

"Why, you bold, lying horse thief!" The Caliph was angry. "You know very well that this horse is mine. How can you think the Cadi will believe your foolish tale?"

"We shall see! We shall see!" said the crafty fellow. "He will look at you, a rich merchant, and at me, a poor cripple whose horse is his only means of getting about. Our Cadi has a soft heart. Like yourself, he will be touched by my old, wooden crutch."

"This Cadi is a wise man, or so I have heard," the

Caliph insisted. "He will soon give my horse back to me."

"Well, I shall be content with what the Cadi decides," the cripple said as he slid from the horse's back.

Before the Cadi, the Kind Caliph, still unknown in his merchant's disguise, told how he had given a ride to the lame man, and how at the end of his journey the ungrateful fellow had claimed his horse for his own.

"The merchant lies, O Wise Cadi," the would-be horse thief declared. "It was I who was riding my only horse to the market fair in this town. I came upon this merchant walking along on the highway. He looked tired and ill. So I gave him a ride. Now, unjustly, he wishes to take my horse from me."

The Cadi looked puzzled. He turned his eyes first on the well-to-do merchant, then on the poor, limping man with the crutch. He thought for a while. Then he spoke thus:

"The horse shall be put into my own stable. Each one of you, in his turn, shall go in and pick out this animal from among the other horses. That will help me do justice in this curious case."

Ben-Assar was the first to enter the Cadi's stable. He walked straight to the stall of his good horse and laid his hand fondly upon its mane.

"This is my horse, O Cadi," he said.

When the merchant had left the stable, the lame man was brought in. But he, too, pointed straightway at the merchant's horse. "O Wise Cadi," the fellow said, "how could you think I would not know my own horse?"

Next morning in court, the Cadi called the merchant and the cripple before him.

"By the laws of Allah," he began, "justice shall here be done. The horse belongs to the merchant. Let him ride on his way in peace! As for this ungrateful lame fellow, let him receive one hundred lashes upon his thick hide. He gave poor return for a fellow traveler's kindness."

No sooner had these words been said than the horse thief threw down his crutch and tried to run from the court. In truth, he could walk as well as you or I can. But the Cadi's men were too quick for him, and they took him away.

That evening, Ben-Assar knocked at the door of the house of the Cadi. This good judge made a low bow when he learned that his visitor was the Kind Caliph himself, instead of a merchant.

"Great is the honor you do my house, Ben-Assar," said the Cadi.

"Greater still is your wisdom, good Cadi," the Caliph replied. "You have proved to me that justice is done in your court. But I would know, if you please, how you could so quickly be sure the horse was mine."

"It was not easy, O Caliph," the Cadi explained. "That thief picked out your horse from among all the others as surely as you did. It was the animal itself that showed me the truth. When you went into my stable, you walked without fear to the horse's side. The horse, in his turn, welcomed you with a whinny. But I saw that the other one dared not go near the animal's head.

"The merchant lies, O Wise Cadi," the would-be horse thief declared.

At his approach, the horse laid his ears back. He drew
up his lip as though he would bite. It was easy to see
which one of you that horse claimed as his master."

"Allah is good!" Ben-Assar cried. "He has given
you rare wisdom. I would that the Caliph may serve
our people as governor as well as this Cadi serves them
as judge."

Such a Kind World

MABEL LEIGH HUNT

OLD GRAY NELLIE was not a handsome horse. But in a kind world one does not need to be handsome in order to be loved. And the orphans at the Children's Home dearly loved Nellie. Since she was too old and stiff to work, Nellie's time was theirs. Being slow, she was safe for even the littlest ones to ride. And on that elderly, sagging back as many as six children could squeeze themselves in a merry row.

Privately, Nellie thought six riders were too many. "Three, now—" she wouldn't have minded at all. "But, by crickey, six squirming, kicking, screeching little orphans! Of course," added Nellie kindly, "they're too young and lively to know how it feels to be old."

And Nellie did have a great deal to be thankful for. Wasn't she spending her declining years in comfort? "An easy, idle life, with plenty of hay in my feedbox and plenty of love from the best sort of people, and that's kids," reflected Nellie. "Of course, not a lavish amount of hay. There could be more, if you come right down to it and state the facts plainly. But no one has any extras in a County Children's Home."

Imagine, then, what a shock it was to her, one cold December day, to look into her box and find it empty!

And, oh, the children felt almost as mournful as Nellie! For Mom Pickett, the matron, said, "It's too, too bad, but the time has come when we shall have to get rid of Nellie. There's no extra money to buy grain for an old horse that can no longer work for her board and keep. So," added Mom, before she thought how terribly shocking it sounded, "I'm afraid we shall have to sell Nellie for fertilizer."

"Sold down the river to the fertilizer plant!" ran the horrified whisper through the Children's Home.

The littlest orphans didn't understand, fortunately. But they heard that Nellie was doomed to go away because there was no food to be spared for her. They saved bits of crusts and apple cores, prunes, scraps of spinach, cooked and uncooked. Secretly and openly they carried these tidbits to Nellie, shivering in the damp December fields where she had been turned to nibble what little grass she could find. The poor old nag, growing more bony every day, was in no mood to turn up her nose and be choosy, though she found prunes hard to get down. And the cheese offered her in the sticky small palm of four-year-old Ruby Mc-Glish made Nellie's mouth feel queer and gummy for hours. Oh, yes, it was a dismal time for all!

To make it worse, Mom Pickett said, "No more rides on Nellie! A horse needs strength for that. Besides, the youngest ones must get used to doing without her."

"Maybe if you just mentioned Nellie—an' every-thing—to the Board," suggested Susan Spitznagle. Susan was thirteen. She had been in the Home a long time—long enough to know that in the hands of the Board of Directors rested the fate of orphans.

"I have a feeling the Board would decide, without a moment's prittle-prattle, that Nellie must go," answered Mom.

"Maybe if we'd drop hints around—to folks in town —and around," ventured Corky Trotter uncertainly.

"We could send an article to the *Bakersville Tattler!*" cried Mickey Malone, who was as smart as they come. "In the article we'd tell how hard Nellie used to work for the Home, and how we hate to see her go to the . . . oh, you know. How the little kids will cry for Nellie! It'd make folks feel awful sorry. Then they'd do something—maybe."

*. . . they carried these tidbits to Nellie, shivering
in the damp December fields . . .*

Mom Pickett smiled at Mickey. "It is a good idea," she murmured. "But there again I'm afraid the Board would think we were behaving in a way not expected of a Children's Home."

But Mickey and Corky and Susan and all the older children thought an item in the *Bakersville Tattler* ought to work magic. They couldn't give up such a promising idea.

"I could write the article myself," declared Susan, who was good in English composition. So, when Susan was not at school, or minding babies, or peeling potatoes or wiping dishes, or dusting, or mending socks, she composed feverishly. Tears rolled off her small, freckled nose as she described with many vivid adjectives the plight of poor Nellie.

When she read the article aloud to the other children, her voice shaking, she could hear long-drawn sighs, sniffles, and choked sobs.

Even Mom Pickett was touched and said, "I do believe there is a future author among us—poor old nag!" Meaning, of course, that it was Susan who might some day become an author, not Nellie, the nag. "I declare," continued Mom, "it seems a pity not to see such a fine article published."

"Well?" queried the children eagerly.

"I'll call Mr. Cox, the president of the Board, and explain," promised Mom, seeing the hope in all the upturned faces. "If Mr. Cox says 'yes,' then the next

time I go to Bakersville some of you may go along.
You may take Susan's composition to the *Tattler* office and present it to the editor. But—if Mr. Cox says
'no,' then that will be quite another matter, you understand," warned Mom.

"Oh, please let Mr. Cox see how important Nellie
is to us!" prayed the orphans at bedtime. So it was
perfectly right and natural to them when Mr. Cox said
"yes." Mom Pickett made an excuse to go to Bakersville the very next day, and with her, as Nellie's cham-
pions, went Susan and Mickey and Corky.

With thumping hearts the children entered the
newspaper office. The editor, his hat on the back of his
head and pipe hanging on his lower lip, read Susan's
composition, while the three orphans waited, tense and
solemn-eyed. When the editor looked up, they could
see twinkles in his eyes. He asked several questions, and
with a thick blue pencil wrote across the margins of
Susan's pages.

"By gravy, kids, this will make a spanking good
story!" he said at last, with a slow grin. "Watch for
Thursday's *Tattler*."

*   *   *

"DO RIGHT BY OUR NELL," SAY KIDS AT
COUNTY HOME
Campaign Now On To Provide Old-Age Pension
For Beloved Old Nag

So ran the headlines in Thursday's *Tattler*. Oh, how the eyes of the orphans lighted up when they read these words and the article that followed! They could talk of nothing else. Happy as she was, Susan couldn't help feeling a bit disappointed that the editor had told Nellie's story in his own way, and not with Susan's lovely adjectives.

"Never mind, child," comforted Mom Pickett. "Editors are like that."

Susan forgot her disappointment in the flurry of events that followed. On the very next day the editor telephoned that the citizens of Bakersville had begun to contribute money for Nellie's groceries.

"We now have four dollars from the Women's Book Club, a dollar and ten cents from some town kids, and eight dollars from the Chamber of Commerce," said the editor. He sounded as excited as any gleeful orphan.

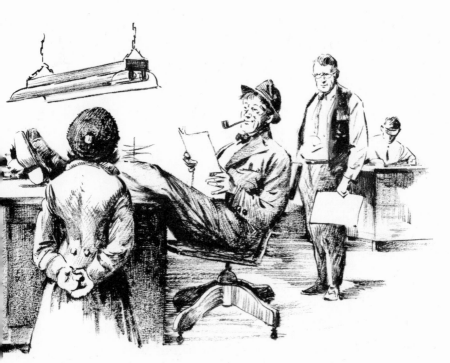

"By gravy, kids, this will make a spanking good story!"
he said at last ...

"That's thirteen dollars and ten cents for Nellie," cried Mickey, doing the sum rapidly in his head.

"Boy, oh boy!" exclaimed all the children, full of breathless admiration for everyone. For Mickey, because of his lightning mental arithmetic; for the editor, because he was so definitely on their side; for Mom Pickett, because she was their only mother; for Nellie, of course; and for the Bakersville folk because of their kind hearts and giving hands.

Susan Spitznagle, carrying a turnip, and Ruby Mc-Glish with a bit of cheese, pattered out to the field to break the good news to Nellie. The old nag pricked up her ears and turning her head politely aside, she let the cheese drop to the grass. "No more of that queer stuff for me!" snorted Nellie in a horsy undertone, "for my future begins to look brighter."

Indeed it did, for the following day an animal doctor came for the one and only purpose of checking Nellie's health. Mom called him a veterinarian, a word nobody could spell except Susan, and she got it wrong the first time. The doctor promised to give Nellie the best of medical care, free of charge!

"The old girl's pretty sound for all her years," he assured the children. "What she needs most is rest, plenty of nourishing food, and at least three loving pats a day. I'll be around now and then to take her pulse and look at her tongue."

He gave Nellie a pill to show that he meant every

word he said. It was huge. Corky Trotter and Mickey Malone promptly went into fits of laughter.

The children were still gazing fondly after the obliging doctor when the postman drove up, chuckling. Among the letters he left was one from New York addressed to Nellie the Nag, County Children's Home, Rural Route 3. When it was opened by Mom, two twenty-dollar bills dropped out! With the bills was a card bearing these words:

From an orphan who knew Nellie
when she and I were young.

Gracious! How perfectly thrilling to know that an orphan could go to New York and become prosperous enough to help out an old friend in need!

"Such things do happen to boys and girls who are good, hard-working and ambitious," declared Mom. "In fact," she went on, as if it were quite an ordinary, everyday thought, "there's nothing to hinder an orphan from becoming President. Or a great writer."

At that, the Home was so full-blown with large, intense, round Oh's and Ah's, it was a wonder it didn't float off its foundations and soar skyward, like an inflated balloon.

Smiling farmers from at least three adjoining counties drove into the barnyard of the Home with corn and hay for Nellie. While these gifts were gathering, there came a photographer from one of the newspapers in

the big city thirty miles distant. He took a picture of Nellie munching, with six orphans astride her. The photograph, which appeared in the newspaper's thick Sunday issue, was explained in large type:

ORPHANS SAVE AGED PET FROM FERTILIZER PLANT

It was the best thing in the paper, of course. There

*He took a picture of Nellie munching, with
six orphans astride her.*

was Ruby McGlish, seated on Nellie's middle, looking squeezed but adorable. Susan Spitznagle perched proudly on Nellie's bony rump. Corky, a little blurry because of wiggling just as the camera's shutter snapped, clutched the mare's scraggly mane. The other three riders were grinning from ear to ear. And to the rueful surprise of Mickey Malone, only half of him showed, standing just inside the margin of the picture.

As for Nellie, crunching contentedly in her warm stall, another happy moment came to her when Mom Pickett said, "Nellie is getting fat and strong again, but the doctor said she must take life easy. So, from now on, children, only three at a time may ride her."

"Okay!" cried every cheerful little orphan.

"Okay, indeed!" exclaimed Nellie, under her breath. "Why, it's a dream come true!" And she reached for such a large mouthful of hay that it stuck out from her lips like cat's whiskers. "By crickey, I'm the luckiest old nag in the world, even if I did look every day my age and not at all handsome in that newspaper picture!"

Nellie stopped chewing and dropped her head humbly, for she was feeling very sentimental and deeply, deeply thankful. "In such a kind world as this," said Nellie, blowing softly through her nose, "one doesn't need to be handsome to be loved. And in my case at least, it all goes back to being loved by the best sort of people—and that's kids."

Washington's Scout

FRANCIS L. KROLL

LEANING FORWARD in the saddle, Jim Watson patted
his horse's neck. "We've made good time, Nig." He
spoke to the horse as though it were a person.

The horse seemed to understand the boy's praise.
Without urging from his rider, Nig turned off the
road onto a path leading through a thick grove of trees.
In a few minutes they came in sight of a small log
cabin. A man dressed in the leather jacket and fringed
leggings of General Washington's Scouts stepped out
from behind a tree. Jim rode straight to him.

"Here's the package the ferryman gave me," he
said, holding out a bundle of clothes.

The Scout quickly unwrapped the bundle and removed a sheet of paper that had been concealed in it. Jim had already dismounted and started for the barn to care for his horse.

"This will probably be the last of these," the Scout called after him. "Howe's army is too close to the ferry for us to get any more messages through that way. In a few days we'll send someone for your horse. You won't be able to use him, and Washington's army needs all the horses it can get."

Jim stopped. He put a hand on Nig's neck. Give up his Nig! If he were old enough to fight, he would ride Nig with the Scouts. Give him up! But with a little catch in his throat Jim knew that he *would* give Nig up if Washington needed him.

Jim fed Nig and carefully rubbed him down before going to the house for his own meal. His mother and the Scout were talking when Jim stepped into the cabin.

"The situation is desperate," the Scout was saying. "The only accurate information General Washington gets is from the messages this lad has been carrying. Now he won't have those."

"If there were some way to delay General Howe's army," Mrs. Watson said, "General Washington might be able to escape with his troops."

"That's right," the Scout agreed, and then he began to talk about people in the neighborhood. Jim was

"The situation is desperate," the Scout was saying.

surprised to see how much the Scout knew about them. He knew the Smiths, the Van Dorns, the Waldens, and that two of the Waldens were with Washington's army. Seemingly he knew everyone. "The Deerings live down by Turkey Creek, don't they?" he asked.

Mrs. Watson nodded.

"They're Tories," Jim said scornfully.

"I know it," the Scout agreed soberly. "That's a job for you, Jim. Their place should be watched the next few nights and we can't spare a Scout."

"It's a long way to the Deering place," Jim reminded him. "I should ride."

"Don't worry," the Scout laughed. "As long as you need him, you can keep your horse."

Jim waited until the sun had set and it was getting dark before he saddled Nig and started for the Deering place. He rode slowly and carefully. Once Nig lifted his head and pointed his ears forward in warning. Jim pulled him aside into some deep underbrush and waited. A rider cantered by. Jim was sure that it was Mr. Walden, but he remained hidden, until horse and rider were out of sight.

Jim had ridden over the countryside many times so he was familiar with the land surrounding the Deering place. There was a low, tree-covered hill on the west side of the farmyard. It gave him a good place to conceal Nig and from there he could watch all approaches to the cabin.

Light was streaming from the few windows of the Deering home. The south yard was well-lit by the fire on the hearth shining through the open door. Jim plainly saw Mr. and Mrs. Deering going about the usual activities of people around a farm. Time dragged slowly past. Jim noticed that they didn't let the fire die down, so they must be expecting company. Of course, that was why the Scout wanted him to watch.

Jim waited as patiently as he could. After a while, he heard the sound of horses approaching from the south. Soon two riders cantered into the Deering yard. Both were dressed in the red uniform of Howe's Dragoons. Jim recognized one of them as Matt Deering. He hesitated, and then he carefully worked his way down the hill and toward the Deering cabin, until he was against the wall. He put his ear to a crack.

Matt Deering was speaking. "We'll be back tomorrow night with a group of dragoons. General Howe wants me to show them the route through the valley. It will be his chance to cut Washington's army in two."

"I'll fix supper for the soldiers," promised Mrs. Deering. "When they chase the rebels away from their farms, we'll get enough chickens and other things to pay for the meals." She laughed triumphantly.

Jim now had important information for General Washington. He worked his way back to Nig, and led him a long distance before mounting. Even then he rode slowly until there was no possible chance of being heard by anyone at the Deering cabin.

When Jim got home, his mother was waiting for him at the door. Briefly he told her what he had learned.

"We won't leave our cabin," she declared stoutly.

"We won't have to," Jim answered. "The Scout will have a plan to stop those dragoons."

But the next morning when the Scout appeared and Jim told him what he had learned, the man shook his head hopelessly. "The few mounted Scouts we have are riding with messages," he said. "There are no foot soldiers near enough to be sent to keep the dragoons from scouting the road. If we had more horses, we would have a chance."

"Take my horse," Jim offered.

"Nay, lad," the Scout refused. "I want you to go back to the Deering place tonight. Learn what you can and report to me at Twin Oaks by midnight. Perhaps you will learn something that will give the General a chance."

"I'll do my best," Jim promised.

Again it was almost dark when Jim left home. He rode to the same hill overlooking the Deering place. Tonight, time passed swiftly. When he heard the approaching horses, he was relieved to see there were only eight horsemen in the party.

The men dismounted, leaving one man behind to

watch the horses. Jim stood undecided. He could report the number of men to the Scout. He remembered the Scout had said he might get valuable information. With the soldier on guard, it would be very dangerous to try to get nearer. While he was still trying to decide his course of action, one of the soldiers shouted from the cabin, "Leave the horses, Smithers. Come in and eat with us. The rebels are all hiding like rabbits in burrows."

Jim smiled grimly to himself. One rebel was hiding all right, but not like a rabbit in a burrow. As soon as the soldier went into the house, Jim crept to the cabin wall.

"We'll look at that valley road tomorrow," one of the soldiers said. "If it's as you say, we'll return to camp and report to the General. In two days Washington's army will be cut in two. The rebellion will be over."

"Maybe we could burn a few cabins on our way back." Jim recognized Matt Deering's voice.

All the soldiers laughed loudly.

Jim started back toward his horse. He had the information the Scout wanted, but the Scout had warned him they had no way to stop the Redcoats. If there were some way to stop this scouting party, General Washington would have time to escape. Jim stopped. If the dragoons didn't have those horses—

He knew it was dangerous to try, but he turned and

circled away until he was behind the dragoons' horses. Step by step he slowly made his way toward them. One of the horses tossed his head and moved restlessly. Jim whispered softly, and as the horses quieted, again moved forward. At last he was standing in front of them.

"Better take a look at the horses, Smithers," one of the soldiers said.

A soldier stepped to the cabin door, took a quick look at the horses, and went back into the cabin.

Jim worked rapidly. He tied the reins of two horses to the saddle of one and the reins of the others to those two. He picked up the reins of the first horse and slowly started leading it. All the horses moved forward. The squeaking of saddle leather and the jingling of metal rings were so loud Jim was sure the soldiers must hear it. Yet he dared not stop.

Slowly the little cavalcade moved away from the cabin. Now they were starting up the hill. Jim became aware of the pounding of his heart. A few more steps— he heard an excited yell from the cabin doorway. "Smithers," the voice roared, "the horses are gone!" Jim heard the dragoons clump out of the cabin. He knew it was only moments until they would spot him He swung himself into a saddle and urged the horses forward.

"There they go," a soldier yelled. "Someone's stealing them!"

There was the roar of a musket and Jim heard the ball whistle past his ear. Another shot whistled harmlessly over his head. The soldiers were being careful not to hit a horse. Now they dashed forward, trying to catch him before he could get the horses running. Desperately Jim kicked his mount in the sides and at last the whole group broke into a gallop. The soldiers began to fall behind.

Again there was the roar of a musket. Jim felt a stinging, burning jerk at his left arm. A musket ball had cut a groove in the flesh. He ducked lower in the saddle just in time for the next ball to whiz over his head. Before the soldiers could reload, he was out of range.

Nig moved nervously as Jim rode up. But he stood still while Jim dismounted from the horse he had been riding and swung into his own saddle. He held the reins of the horse he had been riding and urged Nig forward. The horses followed readily. There were other shots, but none came close.

Jim headed the horses straight on toward Twin Oaks. He knew it was past midnight when he arrived at the appointed place. No one was waiting for him. He swung out of the saddle and stood wondering what to do. He gave a gasp of dismay as a man stepped out from behind a tree with rifle pointed straight at him. Then he recognized the Scout.

"Lad, it's you," the surprised Scout exclaimed, lowering his rifle. "Where did you get those horses?"

Jim told him the events of the evening. When he had finished, the Scout gave an admiring whistle. "You have won a victory for Washington's Army," he exclaimed. "Those dragoons will do no scouting afoot. By the time Howe hears of this matter, General Washington will have his army out of reach."

Very solemnly the Scout laid a hand on Jim's shoulder. "By the authority given me by General Washington," he said, "I hereby make you a member of Washington's Scouts. You will keep your pick of these horses. The others I'll turn over to General Washington."

"I'll keep Nig," Jim said happily.

*"There they go," a soldier yelled: "Someone's
stealing them!"*

Can a Horse Know Too Much?

GENEVIEVE TORREY EAMES

"NO SIR, its like I always said, it ain't good for a horse
to know too much. A horse can be too smart—and that
goes double for ponies. Ponies are generally smarter
than horses to begin with."

John shook his grizzled head and wiped an imagin-
ary speck of dirt from the little Welsh mare's glossy
black neck. Ten-year-old Peter, standing beside the old
man, flung a glance across the stable yard to the big
stone house in the distance. He wanted to be sure that
his father wasn't coming along to hear these doubts
about the new pony. As for her, she tossed her head
and laid back her ears.

"See that, now?" John went on. "She acts as if she heard what I said and felt unfriendly. I'm afraid Lightfoot is gonna make trouble."

Peter looked up anxiously at the man's face. "Oh, John, I think she's beautiful. And you said yourself it was time we turned Mousie over to Susan and got a bigger pony for me to ride. Don't you like her?"

"Never said I don't like her," the old man grumbled. "Only I'm glad your Dad got her on trial, so we can see how she acts. She's a good-looking pony, all right, and she sure can jump. If she had plain pony brains, I dunno where you could find a better pony, now you've outgrown old Mousie." He stopped for a moment and kicked at the soft ground with the toe of his worn riding boot. "But that's just it," he went on more slowly. "She ain't got pony brains; she's got brains like a human, and that's not right. It's not—well, natural."

"What do you mean?"

"Well, the other day when she first came, I turned her out in the paddock to get a drink and she came right back into the barn. She unhooked the grain room door with her nose and walked in and started to help herself to the oats. And that ain't all. I know she's not the first horse ever to get a door open, and maybe she's had experience with that kind of hook before. That's smart, but not too smart. But wait, I'll show you. It's time to feed her, anyway."

He led Lightfoot back to her stall and tied her up. Peter followed, keeping at a respectful distance from the pony's heels.

John brought a forkful of hay and put it in the low manger in front of the pony. Peter sat, chin on hands, and kept his eyes on the pony. Lightfoot pulled at the hay, tossing her head restlessly. She soon had the hay on the floor and started to eat, pawing constantly with one forefoot as she did so.

"Why does she do that?" Peter asked.

"Dunno," John replied. "It's a habit. Lots of horses paw while they eat. Seems to show they're enjoying their food."

"But look, John, she's pawed most of the hay so far back she can't reach it."

"Just you watch now, and you'll see what I'm talking about."

Lightfoot reached back as far as the halter rope would let her and nibbled at the few remaining wisps that she could reach. Then, as if by accident, she slid her right forefoot a few inches forward, bringing with it a small bunch of hay. When she had eaten that, she stepped back a little and again shuffled her feet forward until another mouthful of hay was within reach of her twitching nose.

"But, John," Peter asked in excitement, "does she do that on purpose?"

"She sure does. I been watching her three evenings

in a row. And just look at this now." He picked up the fork and put a morsel of hay over at one side of the stall. Lightfoot stretched out her neck, but the rope was too short.

"Oh, John," cried Peter. "You're teasing her. That's mean!"

John held his finger to his lips. "Wait," he whispered.

Lightfoot reached across with her left forefoot and dragged the tempting mouthful in front of her right hoof and then slid it along the floor to her nose, as before.

"Gee, she *is* smart," said Peter. "Smart as any horse in the circus, I betcha."

The old man shook his head. "Now that's what I say is against nature. A horse paws for excitement or because he feels good, and his legs just naturally paw from front to back. He can't help it. But when he starts pawing the other way, bringing back the hay he can't reach, and using two feet almost like a pair of hands, that's thinking, and not horse thinking either. It's *human* thinking!"

Peter sighed. "I just love her, John. Don't you think she'll be all right after she gets used to me? I mean, it would be just grand to have a pony as smart as that."

John hung up the fork and started for the rain room. "I dunno," he said. "You're a pretty good rider for your age and you can manage any ordinary pony that's not downright vicious. But this one, any time she starts to think up tricks, they won't be ordinary pony tricks. You don't know enough to outsmart a pony that don't think like a pony. Still, you be down here bright and early tomorrow and we'll see how she behaves."

He turned and looked sharply at the boy. "No over-sleeping now. That's for city folks. If you can't get in your morning ride before school, guess we'll have to give it up—give up school, I mean."

But Peter did not ride the next morning. He was up extra early and ran to the stable to help John. "That's right," said John. "You give Lightfoot a drink while I finish cleaning the stalls."

Peter led the pony out to the paddock and turned her loose to drink. Highboy, the hunter, was dipping his muzzle in the clear, cold water in the concrete tank. Mousie had finished drinking and was rolling happily in the dust.

Lightfoot did not go near the water. Paying no attention to the other horses, she walked to the paddock fence. Her head was high, ears forward, nostrils sniffing the sharp air. She seemed to be looking at the wooded hill across the road and she started pacing restlessly back and forth along the fence, keeping her head toward the hill as she walked. For a moment she stopped to scratch her neck against the top rail of the barway that led to the road. The rail loosened and one end clattered to the ground. In a flash Lightfoot jumped the lower bars and started for the road at a high trot. John came to the stable door just as Highboy and Mousie followed her lead, tails and heads high, hoofs flying.

"That pesky pony!" exclaimed John. "Making trouble already, just like I said. Here, Peter, take this rope and follow them. I'll get some oats."

The three horses crossed the road and dashed gaily up the grassy slope beyond. By the time John had joined Peter, Highboy and Mousie had settled down quietly to graze. Lightfoot, however, had not stopped for so much as a nibble of the rich grass. At a fast, steady trot she headed for the woods and disappeared in the fringe of young birches along the edge of the field.

John's face wore a puzzled look. "I can't figure that out," he said. "Can't see why she'd take to the woods and leave all this good feed. It ain't natural."

"Shall we follow her?" asked Peter anxiously.

John shook his head. "Got to get the other two in, first. Can't have them roaming all over the country. Chances are Lightfoot will come back when she finds the others haven't followed her. Horses usually stick together."

He gave a clear, long whistle and began shaking the oats in the measure he was carrying. Highboy and Mousie raised their heads and trotted obediently across the grass to John. He gave them each a handful of oats, and Peter snapped the rope on Highboy's halter. John left Peter to watch for Lightfoot, while he led the hunter back to the stable, with Mousie following behind.

There was still no sign of Lightfoot when John came back. Inside the woods there was no chance of tracking the pony, and not a sound could be heard except the faint rustling of leaves in the treetops. Presently John gave up.

"Looks like the ground swallowed her," he said to Peter. "Anyway, she wouldn't go straight over the mountain unless something was chasing her. She'll most likely take it easy along the side of the hill and gradually work down into the open."

"What do we do now?" asked Peter.

"Guess you'll have to run along to school. I'll take Highboy, later, and go looking in the clearing along

the base of the hill. Most likely I'll have her back by the time you get home."

But Lightfoot was still missing that afternoon, and John was grumbling about his wasted day. "That pony's more trouble than she's worth," he said. "If your Dad takes my advice, he'll take her right back where she came from. That is, if we ever do find her."

Peter could eat hardly any supper that evening. Nobody had a good word to say for Lightfoot, and he knew his father was annoyed and worried. His mother had telephoned an advertisement to the paper and had notified the police and the State Troopers. Yet no word had come in about a stray black pony.

In a flash Lightfoot jumped the lower bars and started for the road at a high trot.

The next day was Saturday. There was no school for Peter, and his father stayed home from the office to help with the search.

"It's hard to know where to look," he said to John. "I can't imagine any horse going over that steep ridge if she didn't have to, and you say you've looked in all the likely places on this side."

"That's right, Mr. Davis," John answered. "There's hundreds of acres of woods along that ridge, but she wouldn't stay in the woods, and I've scoured the clearings and meadows all the way to Edgehill Station."

"You know what I think?" asked Peter suddenly. "I think she went straight over the mountain. She was headed that way and she was going fast. I don't think she'd stop for anything. She acted as if she had something on her mind."

The two men turned to look at Peter. "Could be you're right, at that," said John. "We've been trying to figger what an ordinary horse would do, and she's not ordinary. Yes, sir, I'll bet she had something on her mind—some deviltry no ordinary horse could think of."

Mr. Davis nodded. "Then the thing to do is to take the river road and start searching the farms on the other side. Whose place is directly opposite here? Jackson's, isn't it?"

The men jumped into the pick-up truck and took Peter on the seat between them. In a short time they were rolling along the river road on the far side of the ridge. John stopped the truck at a neat-looking farm-house with the name Jackson on the mailbox.

A tall man in overalls was coming out of the barn. He grinned broadly when Mr. Davis mentioned the word pony. "A black pony, did you say? Yes, I guess I have seen her, and I'll be glad to see the last of her." He led the way around the barn to a pasture gate, and there on the other side was Lightfoot, licking steadily at something that looked like a large white brick.

"Salt!" John exclaimed. "Acts like she's been salt-starved for months."

"But our horses all have salt, don't they?" asked Peter's father.

"Yes, I keep a block in each stall," John answered. "But I hadn't any for Lightfoot when she came, and when I ordered some, the feed company was all out. Said they'd send some in a few days. I never thought she'd be that crazy for it."

"How do you suppose she knew where to come for the salt?" Mr. Davis asked.

John shook his head. "It beats me. I know a horse can smell water quite a distance and I suppose he can smell salt, but this is almost too far away. Looks like she just wanted salt and set out to find it."

"I think that's smart of her," Peter broke in, and he knew at once that it was the wrong thing to say.

"Smart, yes, too smart. That's what I've been saying was the matter with this pony. A horse should depend

on his master and not start out on his own every time
he wants something."

"I don't know how she got into my pasture," Mr.
Jackson said. "She spent most of yesterday hanging
around that salt. That was all right with me, even when
she drove the cows away and wouldn't let them have
any. I knew somebody'd come looking for her sooner
or later.

"But after I took the cows in last night, the trouble
really began. She crashed the pasture gate, nosed around
the pig pen until she let all the pigs out, got into the cow
stable and upset a pail of milk, and then pushed the
cover off the barrel of oats and helped herself. I was
afraid to leave her in the pasture after that, and I haven't
any extra stalls, so I had to put my work-team out in the
pasture overnight and tie her up in the stable."

"Well," said Mr. Davis, "I'm glad we've found her.
What do I owe you for all the damage?"

"Oh, nothing at all. Only I hope she doesn't get away
again. She sure can get into a lot of mischief. I guess
she'd wreck the place completely in three days."

They loaded Lightfoot into the truck and Peter rode
in back with her on the way home. He could not hear
what the men were saying, but he was sure they were
talking about the pony. He was afraid they would decide
to send her back, maybe today, before he'd even had a
chance to ride her.

Unhappily, he pressed his face against the pony's

heavy mane. "Oh Lightfoot," he whispered. "Why can't you be good? If you just wouldn't make any more trouble, and if you'd only, *only* just like me a little bit, we could have neat fun together."

Lightfoot cocked her ears forward. Then she gave Peter a little nudge with her nose. "Oh," he sighed happily. "I believe you are beginning to like me, after all."

Mr. Davis looked thoughtfully when they reached home. "Peter," he said, "I hate to disappoint you about Lightfoot, but it does look as if she's going to be too troublesome. So don't get your heart set on her. If she's going to be too independent, we'll have to send her back and get another pony—one that thinks like a pony, as John says. But since she's here, you can try her out a few days longer."

In spite of John's doubts, the pony behaved well with her new rider, and for several days all went smoothly. John had nailed up the bar-way and fastened all the gates securely, and Lightfoot had no chance to escape.

Every morning Peter and John took a ride before breakfast. Peter loved the little mare and he was proud of her. He looked back on the days when he had ridden Mousie as if they had been ages ago. Mousie was all right for his little sister; she was only five. He saw nothing out of the way in Lightfoot's knowing more than most horses. It was what he expected of her.

Peter was learning to jump. When he and John took

their morning rides they sometimes rode across the fields, jumping the stone walls and fences whenever they came to a low place. Peter was not quite sure of himself. It was fun and thrilling and just a little scary, too.

One morning they had started earlier than usual and were riding over strange country. It was near the end of the week and nothing more had been said about sending Lightfoot back. Peter was beginning to hope his father would decide to keep her.

There was a touch of frost in the air and the horses danced and fretted with eagerness. Peter's eyes were shining and his cheeks were red from the cold air. He was gaining confidence every day. "Race you across the field!" he cried, and was yards away before John could answer.

John touched his heels to the old hunter's sides and galloped easily after the pony. They slowed up as they came to the edge of the field. There was a low wall between them and a hilly pasture lot on the other side. The pony popped over and the hunter took it in his stride.

John pulled up a little. "That's enough," he called. "It's bad going here—got to take it easy." But Peter was away again, faster than ever. Maybe he hadn't heard, or perhaps, as was more likely, Lightfoot had decided things for herself.

John hesitated. His horse could overtake the pony

*"Oh, Lightfoot," he whispered. "Why can't
you be good? . . .*

easily on the flat, but the pony had the advantage on this rocky hillside. If it were a runaway, it would only make her run faster to hear the hunter galloping behind He pulled Highboy to a slow trot and watched anxiously. It was too late now to catch up with them. He could only follow at a distance, hoping and praying.

Peter did not seem to be trying to stop, and Lightfoot ran as if she intended to go for miles. They came to the edge of the pasture at last, where a low wall ran along the top of a steep bank. Below was an old lane, unused except for bringing cattle in from pasture. Lightfoot went over the wall and dropped out of sight in the lane.

John, riding faster now, caught sight of her a few seconds later as he reached the wall. He slid from the big horse and left him standing with reins dangling. He scrambled down the bank on the other side, his knees trembling and his voice shaking with fear. "You stay right there, Peter," he called. "Don't you move. I'll get you out. I'll get you out."

Someone had been pulling down the old barbed wire from the pasture fences and had left it—a great, wicked, jagged heap—in the lane, to be picked up and hauled away by a truck. Into the heap, which she could not see until it was too late to stop, Lightfoot had jumped. The long, snake-like coils wound around her legs and over her back. The barbs bit into her skin.

Peter, thoroughly frightened, clung to her mane. He

would be in the midst of the wire if he got off. He was in just as much danger if he stayed on and the pony should begin to struggle.

John was at the edge of the wire, pulling at it with his bare hands, trying to loosen some of the strands so he could get near enough to lift Peter down.

"Don't you move, little pony," he said. "Don't you start threshing around—not yet. Just give us a chance here." His trembling fingers tore at the wire. Like something alive, it fastened its teeth in his clothes and held him.

Lightfoot looked at the old man with her wide-set, intelligent eyes. Then she turned her head and looked about her, on each side and behind her. Then she did a surprising thing. Slowly and carefully she picked up one foot, found it free of the wire, and put it down in a clear spot a few inches to the rear. One after another she moved each of her feet, inching slowly backward, pausing to see her way. Once she seemed to step deliberately on a strand of wire, holding it down while she moved her other foot.

John stopped wrestling with the wire and held his breath to watch. Then he called softly, "Put your head down against her neck, Peter." Peter obeyed and shut his eyes, clasping his arms about her neck.

At last the pony's hind legs were free, but still John did not move. The wire was still snarled about her knees. There was a chance that she might start to jump and struggle, horse-fashion, and throw herself and Peter into its coils. But Lightfoot took another careful backward step and another, and they were clear.

Breathing a deep sigh of relief, John pulled his clothes loose from the wire and went around to Lightfoot's head. When he had led her out into the lane, well away from the wire, he looked Peter over carefully. A slight scratch on one hand was all he could find. Lightfoot had a few cuts about her legs, but nothing serious.

Highboy had gone home, but John did not mind. Peter would not ride while John walked, so together

they led Lightfoot slowly back across the hills, talking as they went. The pony's ears twitched back and forth as if she understood what they were saying about her.

"I reckon," John was saying, "I reckon a horse can't know too much, after all. Any other horse I ever saw would have threshed around till she had herself, and you, too, all torn to bits. But this pony, she's different. She don't think like a pony, she thinks like a human."

"Sure thing," said Peter. "I knew it all the time." And he laughed aloud. For now he knew that Lightfoot was his for good.

One after another she moved each of her feet, inching slowly backward.

A Grown-Up Could Hardly Have Stood It

LINCOLN STEFFENS

WHAT INTERESTED ME in our new neighborhood was not the school, nor the room I was to have in the house all to myself but the stable which was built back of the house. My father let me direct the making of a stall, a little smaller than the other stalls, for my pony, and I prayed and hoped and my sister Lou believed that that meant that I would get the pony, perhaps for Christmas. I pointed out to her that there were three other stalls and no horses at all. This I said in order that she should answer it. She could not. My father, sounded, said that some day we might have horses and a cow; meanwhile a stable added to the value of a house. "Some day" is a pain to a boy who lives in and knows only "now." My good little sisters, to comfort me, remarked that Christmas was always coming and grown-ups were always talking about it, asking you what you wanted and then giving you what they wanted you to have. Though everybody knew what I wanted, I told them all again. My mother knew that I told God, too, every night: I wanted a pony, and to make sure that they understood, I declared that I wanted nothing else.

"Nothing but a pony?" my father asked.

"Nothing," I said.

"Not even a pair of high boots?"

That was hard. I did want boots, but I stuck to the pony. "No, not even boots."

"Nor candy? There ought to be something to fill your stocking with, and Santa Claus can't put a pony into a stocking."

That was true, and he couldn't lead a pony down the chimney either. But no. "All I want is a pony," I said. "If I can't have a pony, give me nothing, nothing."

Now I had been looking myself for the pony I wanted, going to sales stables, inquiring of horsemen, and I had seen several that would do. My father let me "try" them. I tried so many ponies that I was learning fast to sit on a horse. I chose several, but my father always found some fault with them. I was in despair.

*. . . on Christmas Eve I hung up my stocking
along with my sisters' . . .*

When Christmas was at hand I had given up all hope of a pony, and on Christmas Eve I hung up my stocking along with my sisters', of whom, by the way, I now had three. I haven't mentioned them or their coming because, you understand, they were girls, and girls, young girls, counted for nothing in my manly life. They did not mind me either; they were so happy that Christmas Eve that I caught some of their merriment. I speculated on what I'd get; I hung up the biggest stocking I had, and we all went reluctantly to bed to wait till morning. Not to sleep; not right away. We were told that we must not only sleep promptly, we must not wake up till seven-thirty the next morning—or if we did, we must not go to the fireplace for our Christmas presents. Impossible.

We did sleep that night, but we woke up at six a.m. We lay in our beds and debated whether to obey till, say, half-past six. Then we bolted. I don't know who started it, but there was a rush. We all disobeyed; we raced to disobey and get first to the fireplace in the front room downstairs. And there they were, the gifts, all sorts of wonderful things, mixed-up piles of presents; only, as I disentangled the mess, I saw that my stocking was empty; it hung limp; not a thing in it; and under and around it—nothing. My sisters had knelt down, each by her pile of gifts; they were squealing with delight, till they looked up and saw me standing there in my nightgown with nothing. They left their piles to come to me and look with me at my empty place. Nothing. They felt my stocking; nothing.

I don't remember whether I cried at that moment, but my sisters did. Then ran with me back to my bed, and there we all cried till I became indignant. That helped some. I got up, dressed, and driving my sisters away, I went alone out into the yard, down to the stable, and there, all by myself, I wept. My mother came out to me by and by; she found me in my pony stall, sobbing on the floor, and she tried to comfort me. But I heard my father outside; he had come part way with her, and she was having some sort of angry quarrel with him. She tried to comfort me; besought me to come to breakfast. I could not; I wanted no comfort and no breakfast. She left me and went on into the house with sharp words for my father.

I don't know what kind of a breakfast the family had. My sisters said it was "awful." They were ashamed to enjoy their own toys. They came to me, and I was rude. I ran away from them. I went around to the front of the house, sat down on the steps, and, the crying over, I ached. I was wronged, I was hurt—I can feel now what I felt then, and I am sure that if one could see the wounds upon our hearts, there would be found still upon mine a scar from that terrible Christmas morning. And my father, the practical joker, he must have been hurt too, a little. I saw him looking out of the window. He was watching me or something for an hour or two, drawing back the curtain ever so little lest I catch him, but I saw his face, and I think I can see now the anxiety upon it, the worried impatience.

After—I don't know how long—surely an hour or two—I was brought to the climax of my agony by the sight of a man riding a pony down the street, a pony and a brand-new saddle, the most beautiful saddle I ever saw, and it was a boy's saddle; the man's feet were not in the stirrups, his legs were too long. The outfit was perfect; it was the realization of all my dreams, the answer to all my prayers. A fine new bridle, with a light curb bit. And the pony! As he drew near, I saw that the pony was really a small horse, what we called an Indian pony, a bay, with black mane and tail, and one white foot and a white star on his forehead. For such a horse as that I would have given, I could have forgiven, anything.

But the man, a dishevelled fellow with a blackened eye and a fresh-cut face, came along, reading the numbers on the houses, and, as my hopes—my impossible hopes—rose, he looked at our door and passed by, he and the pony, and the saddle and the bridle. Too much. I fell upon the steps, and having wept before, I broke now into such a flood of tears that I was a floating wreck when I heard a voice.

"Say, kid," it said, "do you know a boy called Lennie Steffens?"

"Say kid, do you know a boy called Lennie Steffens?"

I looked up. It was the man on the pony, back again at our horse block.

"Yes," I spluttered through my tears. "That's me."

"Well," he said, "then this is your horse. I've been looking all over for you and your house. Why don't you put your number where it can be seen?"

"Get down," I said, running out to him.

He went on saying something about "ought to have got here at seven o'clock; told me to bring the nag here and tie him up to your post and leave him for you. But I got into a drunk—and a fight—and a hospital, and——"

"Get down," I said.

He got down, and he boosted me up to the saddle. He offered to fit the stirrups for me, but I didn't want him to. I wanted to ride.

"What's the matter with you?" he said angrily. "What you crying for? Don't you like the horse? He's a dandy, this horse. I know him of old. He's fine at cattle; he'll drive 'em home."

I hardly heard, I could scarcely wait, but he persisted. He adjusted the stirrups, and then, finally, off I rode slowly, at a walk, so happy, so thrilled, that I did not know what I was doing. I did not look back at the house or the man, I rode off up the street, taking note of everything—of the reins, of the pony's long mane, of the carved leather saddle. I had never seen anything so beautiful. And mine! I was going to ride up past

Miss Kay's house. But I noticed on the horn of the saddle some stains like raindrops, so I turned and trotted home, not to the house but to the stable. There was the family, father, mother, sisters, all working for me, all happy. They had been putting in place the tools of my new business: blankets, curry-comb, brush, pitchfork—everything, and there was hay in the loft.

"What did you come back so soon for?" somebody asked. "Why didn't you go on riding?"

I pointed to the stains. "I wasn't going to get my new saddle rained on," I said. And my father laughed. "It isn't raining," he said. "Those are not raindrops."

"They are tears," my mother gasped, and she gave my father a look which sent him off to the house. Worse still, my mother offered to wipe away the tears still running out of my eyes. I gave her such a look as she had given him, and she went off after my father, drying her own tears. My sisters remained and we all unsaddled the pony, put on his halter, led him to his stall, tied and fed him. It began really to rain, so all the rest of that memorable day we curried and combed that pony. The girls plaited his mane, forelock and

There was the family, father, mother, sisters,
all working for me . . .

tail, while I pitchforked hay to him and curried and brushed, curried and brushed. For a change we brought him out to drink; we led him up and down, blanketed like a race-horse; we took turns at that. But the best, the most inexhaustible fun, was to clean him. When we went reluctantly to our midday Christmas dinner we all smelt of horse, and my sisters had to wash their faces and hands. I was asked to, but I wouldn't, until my mother bade me look in the mirror. Then I washed up—quick. My face was caked with the muddy lines of tears that had coursed over my cheeks to my mouth. Having washed away that shame, I ate my dinner, and as I ate I grew hungrier and hungrier. It was my first meal that day, and as I filled up on the turkey and stuffing, the cranberries and the pies, the fruit and the nuts—as I swelled, I could laugh. My mother said I still choked and sobbed now and then, but I laughed, too; I saw and enjoyed my sisters' presents till—I had to go out and attend to my pony, who was there, really and truly there, the promise, the beginning, of a happy double life. And—I went and looked to make sure— there was the saddle, too, and the bridle.

But that Christmas, which my father had planned so carefully, was it the best or the worst I ever knew? He often asked me that; I could never answer as a boy. I think now that it was both. It covered the whole distance from broken-hearted misery to bursting happiness—too fast. A grown-up could hardly have stood it.

The Prince's Foal

FRANCES CARPENTER

LONG, LONG AGO, in a certain kingdom, so an old
Turkish tale says, two babies were born on the very
same day. One was a baby prince, the son of the Sultan,
ruler of that land. The other was a baby horse, the foal
of the Sultan's favorite mare.

When the news of the foal was brought in from
the royal stables, the Sultan said, "My mare has given
our little Prince the very best gift of all. Her colt shall
be the Prince's own foal. Let him be given the biggest
stall in the stable. When he no longer sucks his
mother's milk, let him be fed with the best grain. Let
him early be gentled for the Prince's first riding."

121

From that very day—and even when he was full-grown—that horse was known everywhere as the Prince's Foal. As for the Prince himself, no toy brought him such pleasure as a visit to his foal in its stable.

The Prince's Foal was a horse of great spirit. When the stablemen drew near, he tossed his fine head. He pawed the earth with his hoofs. He pranced and he reared. But with the Prince he was as mild as a young lamb. The child could enter his stall without fear. The boy could even play with the long, silky tail of the Foal without any harm.

The Prince and the Foal grew up together, the best of friends. That little Prince sorely needed a friend, for when he was yet small his own mother died. The new wife whom the Sultan put in her place had no liking for the boy. She was jealous of the love which the Sultan showed for his son. As time went on, the Sultan's wife herself had a son, and at once she began to plot how she would get rid of the Prince.

"If your half brother were only out of the way, my son," she said, "you would become Sultan when your father dies."

Well, when the Prince reached the age of twelve years, he was sent to a school where young nobles learned to be warriors. Each day when he returned, he stopped first in the stable to pat the shining neck of his Foal and to take comfort in his gentle nuzzling.

One day the Prince found the Foal looking downcast. Great tears were rolling out of his soft, dark eyes.

"Why are you weeping, O Foal?" the Prince asked.

"I weep because you are in great danger," the Foal replied. In those fairy tale times horses like this one could talk as well as men.

"What danger could there be?" the Prince cried, surprised.

"The wife of the Sultan wishes to kill you so that her own son may one day have your father's throne. I heard her say to her maids that she would put poison in your bread today. You must not eat it. Say instead that your teacher commands you to go without food for punishment because your lessons were not learned."

So it was that the Prince was saved from eating poisoned food. When his stepmother said, "Dinner is ready!" the Prince replied, "I may not eat. My teacher was angry. He bade me go without food." And even when the Sultan's wife offered to make all right with the teacher, the Prince still refused.

Next day, when the Prince went into the stables, the Foal was again weeping. "This time they will put poison into the evening wine," he said to the Prince. "Drink none of it, O Prince, or you will die."

When the Sultan's wife handed the boy his evening cup of wine, he pushed it away. "Wine makes me sleepy," he said. "And when I am sleepy, I cannot learn my lessons. I will not drink tonight." So once more his life was saved by the Foal.

The next night, the Foal warned him thus, "Do not lie down upon your bed this night. Your stepmother has hidden poisoned needles in your mattress. If they should prick your skin, you would surely die."

So when the Sultan's wife said, "It is time now for bed," the Prince replied, "I shall not sleep indoors this night. My teacher bade us all sleep out in the open as do our fathers when they ride to the wars. I shall sleep on the grass." And for the third time, the wicked woman was bested by the Foal.

The Sultan's wife then gave up trying to do away with the Prince, and all went well for a while. But when he had grown to be a fine young man, she again began to plot how to get rid of him.

This time she pretended to be very ill. No doctor could find out what was the matter.

"It is that I cannot endure your oldest son," the Sultan's wife said. "The very sight of him makes me ill. You must choose between him and me. Send the young Prince far away to some other land. Never let him return, and I shall get well."

Now, that Sultan was a kind man. He dearly loved his oldest son. But he loved his wife, too. She was the mother of his other children. So he gave in to her wishes.

That day when the Prince went into the stable he found his Foal looking sadder then ever before. Tears big as your thumb were rolling out of his eyes.

"Why do you weep, Foal?" the Prince asked ...

125

"Why do you weep, Foal?" the Prince asked, stroking the horse's neck.

"They will send you to a far land, and they will not let me go with you," the horse replied. "But do you pull out a few hairs from my tail. Guard them with care. When danger is near, set one on fire. I will come to your side even if I should have to break down this stable door."

The Sultan wept when he told his son he must send him to a far land. But the Prince replied, "Do not be sorry, O my father. I will go gladly since it is your desire. But I pray you grant me one favor. Give me a fine robe. Let it be blue like the sky! Embroider it with gems that shine like the stars! Make it as fair as the springtime with its flowers! Let it be as pleasing as a summer sea with white, crested waves!"

When the Prince put on his fine robe, he said to his father. "Now am I dressed as fits the son of a sultan."

"You are, indeed, good to look upon. O Light of My Eyes," the Sultan replied. And he wept more bitterly than before when his son went from his sight.

But, before he left the palace, the Prince covered his fine robe with the ragged suit of a beggar. On his head he put a cap of old leather. And he made his face dirty with tar.

Then he went to say good-by to his beloved Foal. Pulling a few hairs from the Foal's tail, he put them inside his fine robe. He kissed the white star on the horse's forehead and said, "Farewell, my Foal. Wait here awhile! When I set one of your hairs on fire, come to me like the wind!"

Off to a far land went the Prince. On his way, one day, he came to the city of another sultan. By the wall of the palace there he sat down to rest.

So it was that the youngest of the Sultan's three daughters looked out of her window and saw him beneath it. Because the day was hot, the Prince had thrown open his beggar's coat. The Princess caught sight of the fine robe beneath it that was like the blue sky. She saw the gems bright as stars. She found it as fair as the springtime, and as pleasing as a summer sea.

"Only the son of a sultan would have a robe such as that," she said to herself. "He pleases me well, in spite of that old cap and the dirty tar on his face."

Now, it happened that it was then the time for the Sultan's daughters to marry. Orders had been given that all the young men in that kingdom should pass the next day beneath the palace windows. The three princesses would look upon them. Each girl would throw a golden apple down to the one she chose to wed.

The two older princesses threw their golden apples to two proud, well-dressed noblemen. But the youngest princess sent her apple straight into the hands of the youth in the worn beggar's suit.

The Sultan was angry. "Surely, my daughter," he

cried, "you do not wish a husband so poor as that one. Try once again."

"This is the one I want," the Princess said. And for a second and a third time, she threw her golden apple straight into the hands of the disguised Prince.

The Sultan, her father, gave in to her wish. The three princesses were married, each one to the husband her golden apple had brought her.

How the people did talk about the poor choice of the youngest of the three princesses! They jeered at his beggar's suit and his dirty, tarred face. And no one jeered more rudely than his two proud brothers-in-law.

The very next day the Sultan fell ill. So ill was he that the court doctors said, "The Sultan will not get well unless someone will bring him the Water of Life."

"Where may the Water of Life be found?" the three sons-in-law asked.

"Ah, that no one knows," was the reply of the doctors. "But the Water of Life the Sultan must have if he is to recover."

The proud husbands of the two older princesses were given fine horses to ride upon as they set out on their search for the precious Water of Life.

"Let my husband go, too," the third Princess begged. "Give him, too, a fine horse so that he also may search for the Water of Life."

They gave him a horse, but it was an old, broken-

*. . . the youngest princess sent her apple straight into the
hands of the youth in the worn beggar's suit.*

down creature that walked with a limp. At every third step, the horse stumbled. Once it even fell down. The proud brothers-in-law mocked the Prince, saying, "How should such a poor fool as that one succeed?"

A little distance away from the palace, the Prince came to a wood. There he got down off the back of the broken-down horse. Out of his pocket he took one of the precious hairs from his Foal's tail. And he set it on fire.

The Prince had only time to take off his beggar's disguise before his Foal arrived. Dressed in his shining robe and riding his splendid steed, he soon overtook his proud brothers-in-law. Following the advice of the Foal, he passed them by. Quickly, he rode to the woodland spring that held the precious Water of Life.

From that crystal pool, the Prince filled a gourd with the life-giving water. For safety, he thrust the gourd inside his fine robe, next to his heart.

On his way back, he again came upon his brothers-in-law. These two were astounded at his magnificent Foal. They were dazzled by his princely robe, as blue as the sky and as bright as the stars. They never guessed that this handsome Prince was the despised husband of the youngest Princess.

"Good day, young gentlemen," said the Prince, reining in his horse.

"Good day, noble sir," they replied. "Pray, can you tell us where we may find the Water of Life?"

"I have just come from its crystal spring," the Prince said. "But I cannot tell you where it lies. As soon as I had filled my gourd with its life-giving water, I rode straight away. So quickly I came that I did not mark the way through the forest."

"Then give us that gourd that hangs on your saddle," one of them cried.

"We are two! You are one! We shall take it from you by force," the other declared. They laid hands on the gourd, never asking if it was the one that held the Water of Life. They would have pulled the gourd off the saddle had not the Prince's horse reared up high on his hind legs, lifting it out of their reach.

"Softly, softly, young gentlemen!" the Prince said. "Since you so greatly desire it, I will give you the gourd on my saddle. But only on the condition that each of you stands still while my horse strikes a gentle blow on your leg."

The proud riders dismounted. Each one stood still to receive a tap from the hoof of the Foal. Neither one knew that this would leave on his skin the curving print of the horse's shoe.

Smiling, the Prince kept his part of the bargain. He laughed aloud as the two rode away with the gourd which had hung from his saddle. For that gourd was filled with plain river water. With one hand holding safe the other gourd inside his robe, the Prince rode on to the place where he had left his beggar's disguise and the broken-down horse.

On this sorry nag he rode into the palace courtyard. His proud brothers-in-law were already off their horses. They jeered at his lame nag. They mocked his beggar's suit.

"We have brought you the Water of Life, O Sultan," the two cried. "We ourselves dipped it from its crystal spring in the forest." They did not mind telling lies.

The Sultan drank the water they poured from the Prince's saddle gourd. But he felt no change. Again, and once again, the Sultan drank, but he was as ill as before.

"My husband, too, has returned," the youngest Prin-

cess told her father. "Truly he has brought with him
the Water of Life."

"How should a beggar succeed when his betters
have failed?" the Sultan said. But he called the Prince
before him.

At the very first sip from the gourd the Prince offered, the Sultan felt better. At the second sip, the Sultan raised himself from his bed. With the third drink,
the Sultan stood, hale and hearty, at his palace window, while the crowds cheered.

"You are indeed my dear son, in spite of your beggar's rags." The Sultan opened his arms wide to the
Prince.

"Then give us that gourd that hangs on your saddle," . . .

*Everyone cheered the young hero as he rode to the
palace upon his splendid foal.*

"If you would have me for your true son, O Sultan, the people of your court must respect me," the Prince said. "I pray you lay down a golden carpet over my road that I may ride to the palace as a sultan's son should."

The people stood on both sides of this golden roadway. The Prince lighted another hair from the tail of his Foal. And once again his magnificent steed was at his side. Off came his beggar's suit and worn leather cap. Off came the dirt and tar from his face. He stood good to look upon, in his fine robe that was as fair as spring flowers and as pleasing as a summer sea. Everyone cheered the young hero as he rode to the palace upon his splendid Foal.

Now it was the turn of the two proud brothers-in-law to receive the jeers of the crowd. For in front of them all, the Prince said to the Sultan. "Uncover their legs, O Sultan. Upon them you will find the marks of my horse's shoes. The brand of a slave was the price these two paid for my worthless gourd of river water. Long will that mark remain to remind them of their false claim to have found the Water of Life."

It was a long time before those stupid ones dared show their faces outside their own homes. And from that day the Prince was the favorite son-in-law of the Sultan. He was named heir to the throne, and in the royal stables no horse had a better stall than his wise, splendid Foal.

No Sum Too Small

MURRAY HOYT

THE WHOLE THING took place in two weeks during the year Jeanie Williams was fifteen years old. For her they were two hard weeks. By the end of those two weeks, when the letter came saying that the thing Jeanie had hoped for was to be given to someone else, she was changed. You did not see the change; she was the same quiet, polite, serious person. But you felt the change. She wasn't a little girl any more after that letter came; she was older, more mature. She was a small adult.

The first day of that two weeks I met her in front of my house. Her face was serious as always, trying to hide the way she felt, but her eyes danced and her step was so light it was almost as if she were dancing.

She said, "Look, Uncle Red—look at this."

She handed me a little magazine called Horsemanship. She pointed to an ad which said that a woman in Massachusetts wanted to find a home for a hunter she wanted to retire, where it would be cared for well and treated with kindness and affection. The woman could not keep it because she did not have stable room and had acquired a younger horse to take its place. She did not want to sell it because she wanted the right to check carefully on the character of the person who got it, and to receive reports on how it was being treated.

Jeanie had been reading the ad as I read it and she said very softly, almost reverently, "It says 'kindness and affection.'" Then she looked full at me and she added a little louder, "It sounds almost as if she was describing me."

I said, "Are you going to apply, Jeanie?"

She said, nodding eagerly, "Oh, yes. Dad and Mother say I can. It's the first time they've ever agreed to anything like that. I told them that if I got it, the money I've saved toward a horse could go for tack, for shipping the horse up here and for the expense of taking care of him. A year from now I'll be old enough to get a summer job that will give me the money to keep a horse another whole year."

I watched her walking away primly, on her way to

school. Under the primness I could sense that terrific excitement that made me expect that at any second her walk might become a dance.

I watched her and I thought that probably Joe and Mildred Williams, her parents, couldn't very well have said anything but yes.

But I knew that it was a mistake. I knew the terrific hurt that was coming to Jeanie when the horse was given to someone else. That magazine was read in horse circles all over the United States. It wasn't reasonable to suppose, even before the letter came, that Jeanie would be the chosen one. . . .

Kids long for things inexplicable to an adult. In Jeanie's case it was a horse. Literally, more than anything else in the world, Jeanie wanted a horse. It wasn't the "Daddy, buy me a pony," sort of thing that all kids go through; it started when she was very small, when Mr. Brown used to put her on old Duffer's back to ride from the barn to the pasture gate, and it grew and grew.

She believed that if you wanted a thing badly enough and worked hard enough for it, you'd get it. And she never lost faith that sometime the good break would come. She was a religious little kid, as much as any kid fifteen years old is religious, and she believed that God would not let her down in this matter because He alone could know how much it meant to her.

We who lived near her were rooting for her because

she was a nice kid, and because I suppose Americans always root for the underdog.

We were practical and we'd seen an awful lot of people with a faith as clear and shining as Jeanie's taste the deep bitterness of disillusion.

She asked for a horse her sixth Christmas when she made out her list for Santa Claus. It was the only item on the list.

Joe and Mildred explained to her that a horse was a very expensive present, that Santa Claus probably knew they had no place to keep a horse, and nothing to feed one. They suggested that she ask for other things in case Santa Claus should feel it best to substitute.

She said, "But he won't do that, because a horse is the only thing I want."

There were some grand presents on Christmas Day. Jeanie was very polite and appreciative. But she grew quieter and quieter all the time they were giving out presents. When they were all through, she disappeared and they knew she had gone somewhere alone to cry.

Joe felt horrible. If there'd been any way in the world he could have swung a pony for her, he'd have done it then. But he was a college professor in the little Vermont college of Mead. During the depression, college professors took a cut and he just didn't have the money to swing it. In addition Mildred had had a lot of hospital expenses when the second child was born, and they were expecting another baby. Joe was paying for his house. And to add to everything else, that house was in a development restricted to household pets. It didn't help much to know that all those things were true when he also knew that Jeanie was somewhere alone bawling her eyes out.

She never asked for a horse again. In fact beginning about then she developed the habit of not asking for anything she wasn't positive she'd receive. She'd go to amazing lengths to hint around and find out whether the answer would be yes before she actually asked. She seemed to dread being refused. That first time must have been very bad.

Joe and Mildred sat back after that and waited for Jeanie to forget the horse business, and they thought this was happening until the tin box appeared on her bureau. It had a piece of brown sticker tape pasted on the cover and on that was printed HORS MUNNE. Inside were her two bankbooks, started by the two grandmothers when she was born, a dollar her grandfather had given her for Christmas, the quarter which comprised her last week's allowance, and a penny which she had found in the big chair after the insurance man had called.

Mildred called Joe in and showed it to him. He looked at it thoughtfully. He asked about the penny and she told him.

He said, "No sum too small."

And Mildred said, "But, Joe, the amount is pitiful and absurd compared to what a horse would cost. She's so ignorant of what she's up against. She's going to be so bitterly disappointed. We've got to make her see just how impossible it would be for a little girl to save that much money."

They waited until the time was right, and then Mildred had a long talk with Jeanie. She explained that Jeanie could not buy a horse for much less than a hundred and fifty dollars. She tried to make her understand how many one-dollar-and-twenty-six-centses it would take to make a hundred and fifty dollars.

Jeanie listened to her and seemed to understand, but the box remained on the bureau, and the next time Mildred looked there was more money in it.

They didn't always know where Jeanie got the money, unless they asked her. But we neighbors knew. It became noised around that Jeanie would, at fifteen cents an hour, do practically anything after school and Saturdays within her strength and ability. And there were a surprising number of errands to be run, trips to the store, hickory nuts to be shucked—things like that. She'd take the nickel or dime, and she'd thank you primly and then she'd start to walk away. Only after a few steps it would be too much for her and she'd run, as if she could hardly wait to reach that tin box.

Mildred saw her put the money in, once. There was really a little ceremony to it. First she opened the box and stirred the contents a little with her hand. Then she held the new piece of money a foot or so above the box to make it clink satisfyingly when it dropped in. After she dropped it, she carefully closed the lid again.

She loved every horse within a mile of home, and some a lot farther away than that. This included several specimens of flea bait definitely not worth loving by any but Jeanie's all-embracing standards.

And all the horses loved her. When she was a little kid still, I used to watch her from my window make a beeline for old Duffer's pasture fence. And he'd trot right over and put his head down to be petted. She'd stroke him and lay her face against him, feel his soft nose. And when he grew tired of this, she'd follow him around and squat beside him to watch him eat. You'd see her lips moving and you knew she was carrying on a one-sided, animated conversation with him. When she was called back to the house, he would follow her to the pasture fence and stand looking after her as she made for home with that sturdy businesslike walk which is peculiar to small children. Duffer never paid any attention to anyone else who came near his pasture.

As the time passed between her sixth and thirteenth years, her character began to take shape. I believed, and Mildred agreed, that wanting this one thing as much as she did probably had a considerable effect in forming it. She was a gentle kid, never cruel. She was quiet, and while she had a grand smile and you knew when

...she held the money...above the box
to make it clink...when it dropped in.

she was happy, she was never boisterous in happiness. In fact all emotion, especially hurt, she hid very successfully from grownups, seeming to prefer to fight it out all alone.

She had a lot of friends but no very close companion as most girls that age seem to have. She was extremely affectionate. She was perhaps more affectionate toward her parents than the average child, and the rest spilled out lavishly among the horses she knew, and among all other animals of her acquaintance indiscriminately.

The Fergusons' horse, Perry, Jeanie rode a lot and fussed with a lot. Mary Ferguson was afraid of it, and Perry was not always completely sold on Mr. Ferguson. The result was that occasionally they could not catch their animal and had to come to Jeanie for help.

Jeanie would walk out there into the pasture and she would call with that serious, grown-up manner of hers, "Perry, you've been a very bad boy. Now you come here this instant."

And Perry would come. He'd trot over with a happy little whinny and docilely allow the halter to be slipped over his head, though a few minutes before he had been galloping from one end of the pasture to the other with a great show of heels when anyone tried to approach him. This I saw with my own eyes. Why it was so, I don't know, unless a horse has some way of knowing who loves him and who doesn't.

She began going out to Helen Blair's when she was ten. Helen Blair lived a couple of miles outside town and owned a stable of riding horses. In the summer she furnished both horses and instruction to a girls' camp on the other side of the state. The rest of the year she gave lessons there at home. Trust Jeanie to find out about a setup like that. The couple of times I'd been out there the place had seemed to be infested with little girls, feeding, currying, saddling horses, and riding endlessly around a ring. And looking at me with polite condescension when I asked what "tack" was and what "posting" meant.

I gathered from Jeanie that, to the little girls who liked riding and horses, it was like a club out there. And they adored Helen. When they didn't have money for a lesson, they hung around anyway.

Jeanie spent most of her time out there. Helen said she used to spend hours just standing in the stalls brushing the horses; sometimes just talking to them.

She took to getting up early and doing her hour of piano practice before school. She'd do her room work at noon, then after school she'd ride out to Helen's on her bicycle. In the evening she'd study and go to bed early so that she could get up for the practicing the next morning.

I saw her out there once and complimented her on her riding. She thanked me carefully. But I watched her eyes. They were looking past me at two girls from the town below who owned their own little Morgans. If I ever read loneliness and longing in anyone's eyes it was in hers then.

When I turned away I knew that with her, the riding, the lessons, the having other people's horses come to her, was all very well. But there was a big, lonely

*Helen said she used to spend hours
just brushing the horses.*

void that only having her own horse to love and fuss over, could ever fill.

I used to ask her once in a while how the horse fund was coming along. Sometimes she'd say, "Oh, pretty good." But sometimes she would tell me something definite and I would know that she wanted to talk to someone about it.

The box was the same one that she had used right

along, but now the HORS MUNNE had been crossed out and over it written, in a little girl's hand, HORSE MONEY.

By the time she was thirteen she was official baby tender for the neighborhood. The money always went into the tin box.

In a way it was too bad she liked ice cream and all kinds of sweets as much as she did because if she hadn't, saving would have been a lot easier. There must have been some pretty hard-fought battles behind that serious little face.

But always the tin box won out. There were only two things that she would spend money on; one was movies which had horses in them (and she saw all of those) and riding lessons at Helen's. Mostly she was able to get her dad or her mother to pay for the riding lessons but sometimes she could not, and then she very reluctantly tapped the fund. By that year when she was thirteen, she had almost one hundred dollars.

That was the year she began to grow tall. She had been a chubby little thing earlier, but suddenly she began to shoot up and all her hems were let out in a desperate effort to keep her properly clothed. I had expected she would be displeased at this sudden shooting upward, but I found her philosophical.

"It's much easier to mount now, Uncle Red."

The fourteenth year was when the pin-up boy appeared on her wall.

"It made me feel old," Joe said. "Here was my daughter starting to put up boys' pictures. It made me feel darned peculiar. So when the time was right I said to her, 'I was in your room today, Jeanie, and I noticed that Roy Rogers is your pin-up boy.' And she said, 'Oh, Daddy, that isn't Roy Rogers' picture. That's a picture of Trigger, his horse.'"

That was the year she found out about an old Morgan that could be had for one hundred and twenty-five dollars and she hinted around to find out whether Joe and Mildred would lend her the extra twenty-five dollars to buy it.

That was a fairly tough decision on all concerned. Joe could have stood the twenty-five without any trouble, but the upkeep he just wasn't financially able to handle. Joe got out a pencil and a piece of paper and he began to write down the things they would need. Jeanie had an old catalogue and they looked up saddle, bridle, and probably other items which I know nothing about. Then he wrote down the everyday expenses that owning a horse would entail. There was stable rental, hay, oats, bran, shavings for bedding, pasture rental; a lot of other items like that. He said that as he wrote, Jeanie's face grew more and more expressionless. The animation drained from it and it became stoical.

They came to the conclusion that they would need at least seventy-five dollars for equipment (which Jeanie called tack) and that it would cost about one-hundred dollars a year—at a conservative estimate—to take care of the horse.

Jeanie saw how impossible it was once the figures were down on paper. She thanked Joe for going over it with her, and excused herself. She didn't appear for a long time. They knew where she was, well enough, and Joe says he and Mildred both felt horrible. Jeanie was older now and very seldom went away by herself any more, the way she used to. It had to be something out of the ordinary to make her do that now.

I saw her a few days later and I asked her how the fund was coming. That was one of the times she told me something definite.

She explained about the cost of upkeep and of tack and everything. She said a little wistfully, "Sometimes, Uncle Red, I get very discouraged. I guess I'm going to be an old lady before I get my horse. I guess it will be so late it won't do me much good."

I said, "But you aren't going to give up, are you?"

And she said, "No, I'm not going to give up." Her jaw seemed to stick out a little when she said it, though that might have been my imagination.

That was the way things stood when the advertisement appeared in Horsemanship. As I have said, by that time everybody knew about Jeanie and her horse, and all of us were rooting for her. Two different people brought her the ad.

Jeanie applied. It was a nice straightforward letter

with only a few misspelled words. Spelling had never been Jeanie's forte.

The weakness in the letter lay in the fact that Jeanie could not describe either the stable or the pasture, but had to say that if the horse were given to her she would have to look around and hire each of these items.

After the letter went off, everyone concerned sat back and waited. I'd see Jeanie walking to school and back and I could see the tremendous excitement in her. She tried as always to hide any emotion she felt, but this was something out of the ordinary so that I could see it in the way she skipped along, in the way her eyes sparkled, in every move she made.

And my heart went out to her because I knew she couldn't win; I knew she couldn't because I was practical and figured the odds; they were many times a hundred to one against her.

She began to get together tack. She bought a pail to water the horse. She went down to the feed store and found out about oats and bran. She canvassed the street nearest our development for a stable. She poked into old barns, carriage houses, stalls. Everything is new in our development, but on Middle Street, which is next to ours, the houses have been there, many of them, for over a hundred years. Some of them have large barns and stables. She finally landed one of these. Then she went looking for a pasture. She spent two or three days on this. She had trouble finding one near enough to the stable, but she stuck to it in her brave, polite little way and finally she succeeded. You went into her room and you found lists of horsy things she'd have to buy.

You watched the excitement in her and your heart went out to her because you knew that she was building up to a disappointment which would shake her through and through, which would hurt her worse than she had ever been hurt in her life. You sensed that. You wished there were some way you could protect her, you could help her—yet you knew of nothing anyone could do.

When people talked to me downtown I found myself sticking up for her. One man said to me, "That is the luckiest thing I ever heard of. Sitting back and having a horse turned over to you."

I said, "I don't call it luck. In the first place it hasn't been turned over to her and probably won't be. But if it should be, it still isn't lucky. She's fought for it for years. She's had some tough breaks. A good break should be about due her. If she doesn't get this particular horse in this particular way, she'll get another one in a year or so because she's working for it all the time. It's the same sort of luck you might accuse a prospector of having when he's studied and worked for months, even years, and finally finds the gold a little quicker than he expected. It's one of those breaks you make yourself."

The guy looked at me surprised. He said, "Okay.

You don't have to get so vehement about it. If you say so, it isn't luck."

Maybe I was touchy because I hated to see it happen to her. Sure she would get a horse in another year or so. To an adult a year is not very long. To a child it stretches away endlessly. When you're fifteen, a year is a long, long time. I wanted her to have the horse now.

It was during this period that Joe heard her praying. He went in to tuck her in for the night and open her window, and before he stepped off the carpet he heard her talking. Her eyes were tight shut and she was asking God to help her, to guide her. She had done everything she could do; now she needed help. He tiptoed back downstairs without going into the room.

She didn't say much about the mail but she went down to the post office every time a train came in, if she was free. And when she came home from school her eyes always went to the table where Joe and Mildred left the incoming letters.

At the end of two weeks the letter came. It was a short letter. It thanked her for her application but it said that under the circumstances, since she had neither stable nor pasture, the horse couldn't very well be turned over to her.

You didn't have to ask her what was in the letter. She drew into herself, and before she finished reading, her face was a mask. She stood there with the letter in her hand for a little while and once Joe thought she was going to drop it. But then she very quietly handed it to him. She wouldn't let them see her eyes.

She said, and her voice was thin and high-pitched, "Well, I'll have all these things ready anyway, when I do get one." Her voice didn't sound very natural. She was around for the next few minutes but after that they couldn't find her for a long, long time.

I guess Joe felt almost as badly as she did. He came over to see me, ostensibly to get any ideas I could give him, but I guess in reality he needed to get it off his chest. He told me that Mildred had phoned Helen for the same reason.

After Joe went back home I sat in the living room thinking about the hours of baby-tending and the running errands, I thought about the money gradually growing in the tin box on the bureau. I thought about Duffer following her across the pasture. I thought about her catching Perry when nobody else could lay a hand on him. I thought about her first pin-up boy, about her seeing *National Velvet* five complete times and parts of two others. She was just a little girl who wanted a horse very badly. And pretty soon I didn't feel very good inside. This had been her big chance. She had had faith, and having faith she had dropped her guard. Now she was hurt as she might never be hurt again. For my money it was a shame and if nobody could do anything about it at least a try could be made.

I picked up the telephone. I put in a person-to-person call to the lady in Massachusetts. The operator said, "I am sorry, sir, there will be a delay. That same call has just been put in by another party."

So I sat around and waited and I began to feel no better fast. I knew Jeanie would be away somewhere alone by that time, and little pictures of Jeanie in the past five years kept passing before my eyes.

After a while the phone rang and they told me that they had my party.

I told the lady who I was, and then I started in. I told her about Jeanie; what she looked like, all the things I knew about her. I told her about those first rides on Duffer, about that first Christmas, about Duffer following her around, about Perry, about the way she mothered all animals, about the tin box and its slow, slow accumulations, about the capacity to love some horse, pet it, make over it, more than any horse was ever loved or made over before.

I said, "You want care and affection for your horse; you can never find them in such quantity anywhere again." I told her everything. She didn't interrupt me much. When I got through her voice sounded a little different. She thanked me for calling and then she told me something about the horse. His name was Topper. He was a grandson of Man o' War—by Thunderer out of a range mare. He was thirteen years old but still very sound. The only strings attached to her offer were that he must not be hunted, or ridden for hire, and must never be sold. If the person who got him could no longer keep him he must be returned. She said that Topper liked to be petted and would stand for hours and be curried. If he liked you he would follow you around. I gathered that Topper was lonesome, now that his place had been taken by another horse.

I said to her, "They're two of a kind. Jeanie has been lonely for a long time, for a horse to love. And Topper is lonely for a mistress to love him."

After that I hung up. When I got the bill later, the call cost me eight dollars and thirty-five cents. I figured I never spent eight dollars and thirty-five cents that I begrudged any less.

I found out afterward that Helen had called just ahead of me. That Massachusetts woman must have learned an awful lot about Jeanie in an awful short time; though maybe we duplicated to some extent. If I had known about Helen's call I wouldn't have put in mine because I would have felt that as one horse woman to another, she could probably swing more weight than I could. I was just a guy who wanted to see a little girl get her horse.

Joe said that Jeanie was very quiet all evening. In the middle of the evening the phone rang and it was a telegram for her. It said: TOPPER IS YOURS. AM STARTING HIM OFF BY VAN YOUR EXPENSE EARLY TOMORROW MORNING. MAY I COME UP SOMETIME

AND RIDE WITH YOU? And it was signed by the lady in Massachusetts.

Jeanie didn't mean to show how she felt any more when she knew the horse was hers than she had when she had thought it never would be. But she came tearing into the living room, her eyes big. Her whole face shone. Her whole body was light, as if she were hardly touching the ground.

They called me over and she had calmed down by then; but I have never seen anyone look so quietly radiant as she did. Joe said that all the next morning she whistled and sang. He said she was so happy that it was all around her like a halo. It wasn't that she had ever been unhappy; she had always been a happy kid. It was just that she had wanted something very, very badly and now she had it and she was so happy she couldn't begin to contain it.

It had to show itself somehow and so she hummed and sang and whistled all day.

At ten thirty that night Helen called and said that the horse was there and was grand; big and lovable. The next morning I took them out before breakfast, because Joe's car wouldn't start.

She got out there and she walked into the stall and up to his head, and he whinnied a little, softly, and nuzzled her with his velvety nose.

And she stroked him and held her cheek against him.

If Wishes Were Horses

ADELE DeLEEUW

WEDGED BETWEEN Uncle Joe and Aunt Emma and pressed hard against the rail, Stacy watched the sulkies wheeling swiftly around the bend and down the track. The two-wheeled spidery carts seemed to fly over the ground, the horses' hooves thundered in swift rhythm, and Stacy, leaning far out, clutched her bag of popcorn so hard that it broke and spilled.

"It's Mr. McGregor's mare," she cried, turning a radiant face to Aunt Emma. "It's Lady! She's winning! Isn't she wonderful? Isn't she beautiful?"

"Now, for goodness' sake—" In her excitement Stacy had dropped her purse, too. "Pick it up, Stacy, quick."

"Oh, Aunt Emma, not till Lady's won. . . . There.
. . . There! She's past the stand. I knew she would!
Oh, I wish—"

"If wishes were horses you'd have two dozen by
now," Uncle Joe said tolerantly, but Aunt Emma
pressed her lips together. "I never did see such a one
for horses. I don't know why Clara and Dan didn't
bring you up like other girls."

Tears stung at Stacy's lids, and her face felt hot. The
cheering of the County Fair crowd drummed in her
ears, but Stacy, for a nostalgic moment, wasn't there.
She was back home—on the ranch that had been a kind
of heaven to her all her life until tragedy had fallen
like a black cloud, obliterating everything. Mother and
Daddy gone. . . . the ranch taken over by the bank, the
horses sold. Midget and Pete and Saracen and Feather
and Lucky Girl and her own sweet Janey. . . .

Aunt Emma and Uncle Joe had taken her in, been
good to her, given her a room newly furnished just for
her, tried to make her happy. But sometimes a wave of
homesickness broke over her with such force that she
didn't know how she could stand it. That was when
she *had* to talk about horses. . . . the horses she had
known and loved, the ones she was going to have
when she was old enough to work and have a ranch
of her own again. She could never be truly happy until
she did have them. Horses were 'in her blood,' as
Uncle Joe said. But he said it laughingly.

He didn't really understand, he or Aunt Emma. They had never known anything but this small town, the old house with its neat garden, the well-ordered, intimate life of the village. Sometimes Stacy felt that she must stifle if she stayed here much longer in this tame, hedged-about atmosphere. She would take long walks into the country, imagining herself on a horse, riding over the prairie.

It was on one of those walks that she had discovered Mr. McGregor's place. The Mansion, it was called. She had heard the townspeople refer to it. It had been a gloomy house, with porches falling into disrepair, and high grass blotting out the curving drive under the ancient elms. Then Mr. McGregor had bought it, had turned the big barn into a marvelous stable, imported a trainer and two stable-boys, and filled the place with horses.

The trainer's name was Mike O'Neil, the people said. He was a terror. But nothing compared to old man McGregor himself. Rich as Croesus, with a shell like a walnut, and just as bitter. Why was he so bitter with all that money, and all those horses? The townspeople shook their heads. And what was Mrs. McGregor like? Some said she was little and faded; some said she was tall and sad-faced; but nobody had ever had a good look at her. Kept to herself. There was some kind of mystery at The Mansion, of that everyone was sure.

Stacy was remembering all that as she stooped to

retrieve her purse. Suddenly she made up her mind. "Be back in a minute," she said breathlessly.

She darted through the leisurely throngs to the long open shed where the race-entrants were stabled. A little wizened man with leather leggings and a bright blue shirt was leading Lady up and down, cooling her before the rub-down. He was the same bow-legged little man who had ridden Lady in the sulky like one inspired. His face was weather-brown and he clamped a cold pipe between his teeth. His cap was pulled low over his shrewd blue eyes and Stacy could see a close thatch of reddish hair. He looked a little forbidding, but she did not stop.

"You're—you're Mike O'Neill, aren't you?" she asked him.

He did not stop walking. "Sure, and who else? And who may you be?"

"I'm Stacy Landis . . . I live with the Holdens. I—I saw you win the race, and it was thrilling! But I knew you'd win—because you were driving Lady. She's the most beautiful mare I've ever seen. She has everything!"

His narrowed eyes studied her. "Ye think ye know a good horse when ye see one, do ye?"

"I do know. I know horses. And I know Lady's a thoroughbred. She—she makes me think of my Janey. Only she's better. I loved Janey, but of course I know Lady's a finer mare."

He was still studying her, as if trying to make up his mind. "You're a quare one, Miss," he said.

"Would Mr. McGregor mind if I stroked her nose?"

He bridled a little at that. "Sure, and how would I know what's in that one's mind? But he's not here, and I am, and *I'm* the one that handles the horses. So stroke her nose and be quick about it."

He watched her, under his low-pulled cap; watched Lady's ears and the way she stood under Stacy's hand. "You know your horses, I'll say that, Miss. You've a way with you not many has. Now where in the —"

They got no further than that. Uncle Joe, red-faced and perspiring, his face creased with worry, spied her then and shouted, "Stacy! Stacy, we've been hunting the grounds over for you!"

"I'm coming to see you and Lady," Stacy managed, over her shoulder, tearing herself away. Mike said doubtfully, "I don't know about that, Miss—" but she could not be *sure* that was what he said. Uncle Joe had her by the arm, propelling her toward an even more worried Aunt Emma.

"I declare, what got into you, Stacy?"

"Oh, Aunt Emma, I'm sorry, but I had to see Lady. . . ."

"Lady?"

"Mr. McGregor's mare. She won the race, don't you remember?"

"Maybe she did. They all look alike to me."

"Uncle Joe, don't you think I could have a horse—not a wonderful thoroughbred, just a nice horse I could ride—"

Uncle Joe mumbled, "You know we haven't the room."

"We could build—"

Aunt Emma said crossly, "And what about the feed? It's hard enough making ends meet nowadays, with the added expense and all, without your talking about getting a horse. I never heard such nonsense. Come along now; my feet hurt."

They didn't uderstand what it would mean to her. If she had a horse that she could take care of, that she could ride and talk to, it would bring the ranch close again . . . the ranch and the corral and Mother and Daddy—everything that spelled home.

In spite of her determination to visit The Mansion stables soon, it wasn't until Spring that Stacy managed it. Then her Uncle Joe gave her a bicycle. It wasn't a horse, of course . . . but it was motion—wind in her hair—trees whizzing by—cloud-racing—all the things she loved.

She left her bicycle by the side of the road near the McGregor meadows. Lady was in the field, and a dozen others, and three wobbly-legged colts keeping close to their mothers. At sight of them, she vaulted the fence —what was a fence to a Western girl?—and walked across the meadow toward the stable, stopping only to stroke Lady and to make friends with the fuzzy colts.

"Here I am," she told Mike. He looked around a bit nervously; the stable-boys stared at her in wonder.

"How—how'd you get in?" Mike asked.

She told him, and a slow, incredulous grin swept over his lean face. "Hmm, nothin' can keep *you* out, I see."

"D'you mind?" she asked anxiously.

"Not *me*," he answered, rather cryptically. She didn't want to ask him what he meant. "Now that you're here, look your fill," he said.

She wandered over the stable for an ecstatic hour. There were stalls of shining, varnished wood, with iron grill work between. A freshly scrubbed stone floor. High windows through which the spring sunlight filtered. A tack room with silver-mounted harness, glittering in the light, and cases of cups and ribbons—blue and red. Mike would stand near the door for a while, then come and tell her some interesting bit about one of the horses; how some of the prizes had been won.

"Begorry, it's a pleasure to talk with a knowin' lass! The dolts around here don't know a bit of good horse-flesh when they see it, and care less. You're not from around here, I take it?"

"No," she said. "That is, I am now . . . but I was raised on a ranch." And under his sympathetic prodding she told him about the golden days when she had had Mother and Dad . . . and her own Janey.

'Ye think ye know a good horse when ye see one, do ye?'

Stacy and Mike got to be fast friends. "It's good to have somebody to talk to," he told her one day, clamping his unlit pipe between his teeth. "Them boys are no good at all, at all—their minds on nothin' but how to get out of workin'—and Himself no satisfaction eyether. As for Herself—" he gave a shrug. "She's a lady I feel sorry for, I do that."

"Why, Mike?"

He said briskly, "Sure, and I've said too much already." He let Stacy help him curry the horses; let her lead them around the turf ring. She pored over their histories with him, and helped Mike doctor them. It was always hard to tear herself away. Other duties seemed so prosaic after that. "When may I come again?" she'd ask, and Mike would scratch his head. After long thought he would say, "Come Wednesday . . . yes, Wednesday. And mind ye be a good gurrul in the meantime."

The days varied. Sometimes he'd ask her twice in a week; sometimes ten days would go by before he'd issue an invitation. One time there was a dreadful span of fourteen endless days. She couldn't stand it. Lady was going to foal, and she had had no news.

She rode slowly past The Mansion, back and forth, back and forth. Finally, she spurted up the drive. Someone raised a window, and called to her. She had a glimpse of a sad white face. Then the window was banged down with a crash that rattled the glass, and

the shade was pulled. It puzzled her, but as soon as she
got to the stable she forgot about it.

Mike was in a bad humor. One of the stable-boys
was sick—or so he said—and the other was a good-for-
nothing. "I'd fire the both of them," he grumbled, "but
boys is hard to get these days, and I'm too old to do all
the work meself."

Stacy said comfortingly, "I'll help all I can, Mike.
Tell me what to do."

She worked busily beside him, going from stall to
stall and renewing friendships.

"Damon's restless," Mike said. "Needs a workout.
Want to take him around a bit?"

"Oh, Mike!" Stacy breathed, afraid she had only
dreamt it. "Oh, Mike, may I, really?"

He held his hand out to give her a leg up, but she
leaped neatly onto Damon's bare back. Mike whistled
appreciatively. He watched her gentling Damon, and
then out into the sunshine. "You can ride, all right,"
he shouted to her. She laughed with joy. It was wonderful—the feel of a horse under her again, the wind
in her face, the soft thud of Damon's hooves, the sense
of freedom and motion.

She circled the field a dozen times; then suddenly
she saw a tall, stout man bearing down upon her, cane
upraised. His face was purple with rage. She drew to
a halt, and he surged forward shaking the cane in her
face.

"You—you—where did you come from? What are you doing on one of my horses? What does this mean? Get off at once, get off and explain yourself."

She slid to the ground. "I'm sorry, Mr. McGregor—"

"Not a word out of you!"

Mike came running up. "Mr. McGregor, sorr—"

"Nor out of you, either. Get off this place and don't you ever come here again! The brass, the nerve of you! Get off my place, I say! I've a good mind to take this cane to you!"

"Mr. McGregor, sorr—"

"And to you, too, O'Neill! Rank carelessness! So that's what goes on behind my back, when I'm away! I saw this young scalawag coming up the drive. I couldn't believe my eyes!" His face was apoplectic. "Well, what are you waiting for? Get out!"

Stacy pedaled home furiously, the blood beating angrily in her ears. The hateful old man—hateful, hateful! Aunt Emma was horrified when she heard of the incident. "Nobody can talk like that to a Holden or a Landis! Don't you ever set foot on their place—or near it, do you hear? That's what comes of meddling in other folks' business! You and your horses!"

But Stacy couldn't forget that ride. It had brought everything back to her, stronger, more poignantly, than ever. Her days were one long homesickness now, and she didn't see how she could live through the summer. It had been such a lovely thing while it lasted.

She lay out under the apple tree, imagining it was the hay loft; she rode her bike with closed eyes, imagining she was galloping over the field on Damon or Lady. She stared up at the stars at night, saying fervently, "Star bright, star light, first star I see tonight, I wish I may—I wish I might—" And then a long sigh. It was silly to wish. Wishes like that never came true. Never. Not here, anyway.

After that the summer dragged by in an endless succession of monotonous days. The air was hot and sultry, and even swimming did not make her feel right. She rode listlessly down the long road, one day after her swim, her thoughts ranging back to the past. Almost without her volition she found herself turning off toward the McGregor place. It wouldn't hurt just to look over the fence, would it, just to look——?

Fellow was standing under a distant tree; and she could make out Hero and Ballyhoo. But the others must be in the stable. How was Lady, she wondered? And her foal? She must have foaled by this time. Stacy's eyes turned toward the stable, and her heart stopped, then thudded fearfully. There was smoke curling from the roof, and a curl of gray wafted out of one of the windows. . . . smoke on an August day.

Stacy grabbed her wet bathing suit from the bicycle basket and tied it over her nose and mouth, vaulted the fence, and sprinted across the field. The high, whinnying neighs of the frightened horses struck at her ears as she tore through the wide doors. The air was hazy with smoke and the acrid smell of it penetrated even the wet fold around her face. Where was Mike? Where were the boys? She knew what must have happened—someone had dropped a cigarette or a match in the hayloft.

Which horse first? Oh, Lady, of course, Lady and her foal. In the special box stall she found them, Lady's eyes rolling, her nostrils showing red. Stacy flung a blanket over the horse's head, spoke to her soothingly. "Come, Lady, come, Lady. . . ." with one hand guiding her, with the other leading the stumbling little colt. She pleaded and coaxed and pushed. Lady reared and balked and whinnied, but Stacy's calm, urging voice forced her forward, into the blessed air.

She tied them to the stake at the far end of the ring; otherwise, she knew, they would blindly have followed her back. Damon next. . . . a Damon wild-eyed with fear. The smoke was thicker now, her eyes smarted and she felt choked and breathless. The noise of their frightened cries made the stable clamorous. If only someone would help! She could never get them all out in time! What if some refused to come? She mustn't think of that.

One after the other, methodically . . . . "Come, Griselda . . . nice girl. . . ." "Sultan, quiet, Sultan!" One more now. . . . King, in the last stall. He reared as she entered, and tried to throw the blanket off his head. He pawed frantically and neighed in shrill hysteria. The smoke was so thick she could scarcely see him. She strained upward to reach his halter. There were voices outside. "Good glory . . . who took them out? . . . Who's in there? Stacy, Stacy, gurrul, are ye all right?"

But she could not answer. King's rearing head jerked her arm upward and she lost her balance. She fell face forward in the stall, and everything turned black.

"It's that Mike O'Neill to see you," Aunt Emma said, her back stiff with disapproval. "I said he couldn't come in, but you could talk to him out the window."

She pushed Stacy's chair close, and laid a scarf around her shoulders. Stacy laid her bandaged hands on the sill and leaned out.

Mike was holding his cap, his red thatch gleamed in the light. "It's a wonderful gurrul ye are, Miss Stacy, a wonderful gurrul! Mr. McGregor is after waitin' to come and see you as soon as ever he can, and Herself, too."

"I'll be glad to have them," Stacy said. "Is everything all right?"

"It is that . . . in more ways than one. And I was to tell you why he was such a curmudgeon that day and chased you off. It's like his own daughter you are, and ye gave him a start. She died these twelve years ago, a fine lass about your age. He never got over it, nor Herself eyether."

Damon next—a Damon wild-eyed with fear.

So that was the mystery of The Mansion, Stacy thought. Her heart welled with pity for the Mc-Gregors.

"He was gone that day and I to fetch him with the carriage," Mike said. "So the boys went gallivantin'. If you hadn't come along, I don't like to think— Aye, it was Providence, that's what it was. And now wait a minute; I've a present from Himself."

He disappeared around the house, and Stacy could hardly contain herself. What could it possibly be? When Mike appeared again, she cried out, "Oh, Mike, not for me! Not that darling colt for *me!*"

"And who else?" he demanded. "It's Lady's own. Look at them legs, will ye, and that muzzle, and this fine back. It's many a ribbon this one will be winning!"

A colt of her own! To love and care for and talk to! It couldn't be . . . And suddenly her face fell. No, it couldn't be. "There isn't room," she said in a whisper. "And the feed—"

"And who said anything about room and feed?" Mike asked belligerently. "You'll keep it at the stables, of course, and Himself will pay for its keep. Then when you want to ride, there'll be the stableful to choose from . . . and this one for your very own. You're to name her. Now, what will ye be after callin' her?"

Stacy cried, "Why, Janey, of course!" And the ranch and Mother and Daddy were close again, and she was happy as she hadn't been since she had lost them.

The Winged Horse

NATHANIEL HAWTHORNE

ONCE, IN THE OLD, old times a fountain gushed out of a hillside in the marvellous land of Greece. And for aught I know, after so many thousand years, it is still gushing out of the very self-same spot. At any rate, there was the pleasant fountain sparkling down the hill-side in the golden sunset, when a handsome young man named Bellerophon drew near its margin. In his hand he held a magic bridle, studded with brilliant gems, and adorned with a golden bit.

Seeing an old man, and another of middle age, and a little boy, near the fountain, and likewise a maiden, he paused, and begged that he might refresh himself.

175

"This is very delicious water," he said to the maiden, as he rinsed and filled her pitcher. "Will you be kind enough to tell me whether the fountain has any name?"

"Yes; it is called the Fountain of Pirene," answered the maiden.

"This, then, is Pirene? I thank you for telling me its name. I have come from a far-away country to find this very spot."

A middle-aged country fellow stared hard at young Bellerophon, and at the handsome bridle which he carried in his hand.

"The water-courses must be getting low, friend, in your part of the world," remarked he, "if you come so far only to find the Fountain of Pirene. Pray, have you lost a horse? I see you carry the bridle in your hand; and a very pretty one it is, with that double row of bright stones upon it."

"I have lost no horse," said Bellerophon, with a smile. "But I happen to be seeking a very famous one, which, as wise people have informed me, must be found hereabouts. Do you know whether the winged horse Pegasus still haunts the Fountain of Pirene, as he used to do in your forefathers' days?"

The country-fellow laughed.

"Pegasus, indeed!" cried he, turning up his nose as high as such a flat nose could be turned up. "Pegasus, indeed! A winged horse, truly! Why, friend, are you in your senses? Of what use would wings be to a horse? I don't believe in Pegasus. There never was such a ridiculous kind of a horse-fowl made!"

"I have reason to think otherwise," said Bellerophon.

And then he turned to an old, grey man, who was leaning on a staff, and listening very attentively, with his head stretched forward, and one hand at his ear.

"And what say you, venerable sir?" inquired he. "In your younger days, I should imagine, you must frequently have seen the winged steed!"

"Ah, young stranger, my memory is very poor!" said the aged man. "When I was a lad, if I remember rightly, I used to believe there was such a horse, and so did everybody else.

"And have you never seen him, my fair maiden?" asked Bellerophon of the girl.

"Once I thought I saw him," replied the maiden, with a smile and a blush. "It was either Pegasus or a large white bird, a very great way up in the air. And one other time, as I was coming to the fountain with my pitcher, I heard a neigh. Oh, such a brisk and melodious neigh as that was! My heart leaped with delight at the sound. But it startled me, nevertheless; so that I ran home without filling my pitcher."

"That was truly a pity!" said Bellerophon.

And he turned to the child who was gazing up at him with his rosy mouth wide open.

"Well, my little fellow," cried Bellerophon, playfully pulling one of his curls, "I suppose you have often seen the winged horse."

"That I have," answered the child, very readily. "I saw him yesterday, and many times before."

"You are a fine little man!" said Bellerophon, drawing the child closer to him. "Come, tell me all about it."

"Why," replied the child, "I often come here to sail little boats in the fountain. And sometimes, when I look down into the water, I see the image of the winged horse in the picture of the sky that is there."

And Bellerophon put his faith in the child, who had seen the image of Pegasus in the water, and in the maiden, who had heard him neigh so melodiously.

Therefore, he hunted about the Fountain of Pirene for a great many days afterwards.

Now you will, perhaps, wish to be told why it was that Bellerophon had undertaken to catch the winged horse. It will be quite enough to say that, in a certain country of Asia, a terrible monster, called a Chimera, had made its appearance. This Chimera was nearly, if not quite, the ugliest and most poisonous creature, and the strangest and unaccountablest, and the hardest to fight with, and the most difficult to run away from, that ever came out of the earth's inside. It had a tail like a boa-constrictor; its body was like I do not care what; and it had three separate heads, one of which was a lion's, the second a goat's, and the third an abominably great snake's. And a hot blast of fire came flaming out of each of its three mouths!

With its flaming breath, it could set a forest on fire, or burn up a field of grain, or, for that matter, a village, with all its fences and houses. It laid waste the whole country round about.

While the hateful beast was doing all these horrible things, it so chanced that Bellerophon came to that part of the world on a visit to the king, The king's name was Iobates, and Lycia was the country which he ruled over. Bellerophon was one of the bravest youths in the world, and desired nothing so much as to do some valiant deed, such as would make all mankind admire and love him. In those days, the only way for a young man to distinguish himself was by fighting battles, either with the enemies of his country or with wicked giants, or with troublesome dragons, or with wild beasts, when he could find nothing more dangerous to encounter. King Iobates, perceiving the courage of his youthful visitor, proposed to him to go and fight the Chimera, which everybody was afraid of, and which, unless it should be soon killed, was likely to convert Lycia into a desert. Bellerophon hesitated not a moment, but assured the king that he would either slay this Chimera or perish in the attempt.

But in the first place, as the monster was so prodigiously swift, he bethought himself that he should never win the victory by fighting on foot. The wisest thing he could do, therefore, was to get the very best and fleetest horse that could anywhere be found. And what other horse in all the world was half so fleet as the marvellous horse Pegasus, who had wings as well as legs, and was even more active in the air than on the earth? To be sure, a great many people denied that there was any such horse with wings.

Well was it for Bellerophon that the child had grown so fond of him, and was never weary of keeping him company. Every morning the child gave him a new hope.

"Dear Bellerophon," he would cry, looking up hopefully into his face, "I think we shall see Pegasus to-day!"

And at length, if it had not been for the little boy's unwavering faith, Bellerophon would have given up all hope, and would have gone back to Lycia and have done his best to slay the Chimera without the help of the winged horse.

One morning the child spoke to Bellerophon even more hopefully than usual.

"Dear, dear Bellerophon," cried he, "I know not why it is, but I feel as if we should certainly see Pegasus to-day!"

And all that day he would not stir a step from Bellerophon's side. So they ate a crust of bread together, and drank some of the water of the fountain. In the afternoon there they sat, and, when he least thought of it, Bellerophon felt the pressure of the child's little hand, and heard a soft, almost breathless whisper.

"See there, dear Bellerophon! There is an image in the water!"

The young man looked down into the fountain, and saw what he took to be the reflection of a bird which seemed to be flying at a great height in the air, with a gleam of sunshine on its snowy wings.

"What a splendid bird it must be!" said he. "And how very large it looks, though it must really be flying higher than the clouds!"

"It makes me tremble!" whispered the child. "I am afraid to look up into the air! Dear Bellerophon, do you not see that it is no bird? It is the winged horse Pegasus!"

Bellerophon's heart began to throb! He caught the child in his arms, and shrank back with him, so that they were both hidden among the thick shrubbery which grew all around the fountain.

Nearer and nearer came the aerial wonder. Downward came Pegasus, in wide, sweeping circles, which grew narrower and narrower still as he approached the earth. At last, with so slight a pressure as hardly to bend the grass about the fountain, he alighted, and, stooping his wild head, began to drink.

After drinking to his heart's content, the winged horse began to caper to and fro and dance, as it were out of mere idleness and sport.

At length, Pegasus folded his wings, and lay down

on the soft green turf. But, being too full of aerial life to remain quiet for many moments together, he soon rolled over on his back, with his four slender legs in the air.

Finally, when he had had enough of rolling over and over, Pegasus turned himself about, and, indolently, like any other horse, put out his fore-legs, in order to rise from the ground; and Bellerophon, who had guessed that he would do so, darted suddenly from the thicket, and leaped astride of his back.

Yes, there he sat, on the back of the winged horse!

But what a bound did Pegasus make, when, for the first time, he felt the weight of a mortal man upon his loins! Before he had time to draw a breath, Bellerophon found himself five hundred feet aloft, and still shooting upward, while the winged horse snorted and trembled with terror and anger. Upward he went, up, up, up, until he plunged into the cold misty bosom of a cloud.

He skimmed straight forward, and sideways, and backward. He reared himself erect, with his fore-legs on a wreath of mist, and his hind-legs on nothing at all. He flung out his heels behind, and put down his head between his legs, with his wings pointing right upward. At about two miles' height above the earth, he turned a somersault, so that Bellerophon's heels were where his head should have been, and he seemed to look down into the sky, instead of up. He twisted his head about, and looking Bellerophon in the face, with fire flashing from his eyes, made a terrible attempt to bite him. He fluttered his pinions so wildly that one of the silver feathers was shaken out, and floating earthward, was picked up by the child, who kept it as long as he lived, in memory of Pegasus and Bellerophon.

But the latter (who, as you may judge, was as good a horseman as ever galloped) had been watching his opportunity, and at last clapped the golden bit of the enchanted bridle between the winged steed's jaws. No sooner was this done than Pegasus became as manageable as if he had taken food all his life out of Bellerophon's hand.

While Pegasus had been doing his utmost to shake Bellerophon off his back, he had flown a very long distance; and they had come within sight of a lofty mountain by the time the bit was in his mouth. Bellerophon had seen this mountain before, and knew it to be Helicon, on the summit of which was the winged horse's abode. Thither Pegasus now flew, and, alighting, waited patiently until Bellerophon should please to dismount. The young man, accordingly, leaped from the steed's back, but still held him fast by the bridle. Meeting his eyes, however, he was so affected by the thought of the free life which Pegasus had heretofore lived, that he could not bear to keep him a prisoner if he really desired his liberty.

Obeying this generous impulse, he slipped the enchanted bridle off the head of Pegasus.

"Leave me, Pegasus!" said he. "Either leave me, or love me."

In an instant, the winged horse shot almost out of sight, soaring straight upward from the summit of Mount Helicon. Ascending higher and higher, he looked like a bright speck, and at last could no longer be seen in the hollow waste of the sky. And Bellerophon was afraid that he should never behold him more. But, while he was lamenting his own folly, the bright speck reappeared, and drew nearer and nearer, until it descended lower than the sunshine; and behold, Pegasus had come back! After this, there was no more fear of the winged horse making his escape. He and Bellerophon were friends, and put loving faith in one another.

That night they lay down and slept together, with Bellerophon's arm about the neck of Pegasus.

In this manner, Bellerophon and the wondrous steed spent several days, and grew better acquainted and fonder of each other all the time. They went on long journeys, and sometimes ascended so high that the earth looked hardly bigger than—the moon. They visited distant countries, and amazed the inhabitants. A thousand miles a day was no more than an easy space for the fleet Pegasus to pass over. Bellerophon was delighted with this kind of life, and would have liked nothing better than to live always in the same way, but he could not forget the horrible Chimera, which he had promised King Iobates to slay. So, at last, when he had become well accustomed to feats of horsemanship in the air, and could manage Pegasus with the least motion of his hand, and had taught him to obey his voice, he determined to attempt the performance of this perilous adventure.

He then turned the head of Pegasus towards the east, and set out for Lycia. In their flight they overtook an eagle, and came so nigh him, before he could get out of their way, that Bellerophon might easily have caught him by the leg. Hastening onward at this rate, it was still early in the forenoon when they beheld the lofty mountains of Lycia,

There was nothing remarkable to be detected, at first sight, in any of the valleys and dells that lay among the precipitous heights of the mountains. Nothing at all; unless, indeed, it were three spires of black smoke, which issued from what seemed to be the mouth of a cavern, and clambered sullenly into the atmosphere.

Bellerophon made a sign, which the winged horse understood, and sunk slowly through the air, until his hoofs were scarcely more than a man's height above the rocky bottom of the valley. In front, as far off as you could throw a stone, was the cavern's mouth,

There seemed to be a heap of strange and terrible creatures curled up within the cavern. Their bodies lay so close together that Bellerophon could not distinguish them apart; but, judging by their heads, one of these creatures was a huge snake, the second a fierce lion, and the third an ugly goat. The lion and the goat were asleep; the snake was broad awake, and kept staring about him with a great pair of fiery eyes. But— and this was the most wonderful part of the matter— the three spires of smoke evidently issued from the nostrils of these three heads! So strange was the spectacle, that, though Bellerophon had been expecting it, the truth did not immediately occur to him that here was the terrible three-headed Chimera.

Pegasus sent forth a neigh that sounded like the call of a trumpet to battle. At this sound the three heads reared themselves erect, and belched out great flashes of flame. Before Bellerophon had time to consider what to do next, the monster flung itself out of the cavern and sprung straight towards him, with its immense claws extended, and its snaky tail twisting itself venomously behind. If Pegasus had not been as nimble as a bird, both he and his rider would have been overthrown by the Chimera's headlong rush, and thus the battle have been ended before it was well begun. But the winged horse was not to be caught so. In the twinkling of an eye he was up aloft, half way to the clouds, snorting with anger.

The Chimera, on the other hand, raised itself up so as to stand absolutely on the tip-end of its tail, with

its talons pawing fiercely in the air, and its three heads
spluttering fire at Pegasus and his rider. Bellerophon,
meanwhile, was fitting his shield on his arm, and drawing his sword.

"Now, my beloved Pegasus," he whispered in the
winged horse's ear, "thou must help me to slay this in-
sufferable monster; or else thou shalt fly back to thy
solitary mountain peak without thy friend Bellerophon.

Pegasus whinnied, and, turning back his head,
rubbed his nose tenderly against his rider's cheek.

"I thank you, Pegasus," answered Bellerophon.
"Now, then, let us make a dash at the monster!"

Uttering these words, he shook the bridle; and Pegasus darted down aslant, as swift as the flight of an
arrow; right towards the Chimera's three-fold head,
which all this time was poking itself as high as it could
into the air. As he came within arm's length, Bellerophon made a cut at the monster, but was carried onward by his steed before he could see whether the
blow had been successful.

Pegasus continued his course, but soon wheeled
round, at about the same distance from the Chimera
as before. Bellerophon then perceived that he had cut
the goat's head of the monster almost off, so that it
dangled downward by the skin, and seemed quite dead.

But, to make amends, the snake's head and the lion's
head had taken all the fierceness of the dead one into

themselves, and spit flame, and hissed, and roared, with a vast deal more fury than before.

"Never mind, my brave Pegasus!" cried Bellerophon. "With another stroke like that, we will stop either its hissing or its roaring."

And again he shook the bridle. Dashing aslantwise as before, the winged horse made another arrow-flight towards the Chimera, and Bellerophon aimed another downright stroke at one of the two remaining heads as he shot by. But this time neither he nor Pegasus escaped so well as at first. With one of its claws the Chimera had given the young man a deep scratch on his shoulder, and had slightly damaged the left wing of the flying steed with the other. On his part Bellerophon had mortally wounded the lion's head of the monster, insomuch that it now hung downward, with its fire almost extinguished, and sending out gasps of thick black smoke.

"Dost thou bleed, my immortal horse?" cried the young man, caring less for his own hurt than for the anguish of this glorious creature, that ought never to have tasted pain. "The execrable Chimera shall pay for this mischief with his last head!"

Then he shook the bridle, shouted loudly, and guided Pegasus not slantwise as before, but straight at the monster's hideous front. So rapid was the onset, that it seemed but a dazzle and a flash before Bellerophon was at close grips with his enemy.

The Chimera, by this time, after losing its second head, had got into a red-hot passion of pain and rampant rage. It so flounced about, half on earth and partly in the air, that it was impossible to say which element it rested upon. It opened its snake-jaws to such an abominable width that Pegasus might almost have flown right down its throat, wings outspread, rider and all! At their approach it shot out a tremendous blast of its fiery breath, and enveloped Bellerophon and his steed in a perfect atmosphere of flame, singeing the wings of Pegasus, scorching off one whole side of the young man's golden ringlets.

But this was nothing to what followed.

When the airy rush of the winged horse had brought him within the distance of a hundred yards, the Chimera gave a spring, and flung its huge, awkward, venomous, and utterly detestable carcass right upon poor Pegasus, clung round him with might and main, and tied up his snaky tail into a knot! Up flew the aerial steed, higher, higher, higher, above the mountain peaks, above the clouds, and almost out of sight of the solid earth. But still the earth-born monster kept its hold, and was borne upward, along with the creature of light and air.

Bellerophon, meanwhile, turning about, found himself face to face with the ugly grimness of the Chimera's visage, and could only avoid being scorched to death, or bitten right in twain, by holding up his shield.

But still the earth-born monster kept its hold...

Over the upper edge of the shield he looked sternly into the savage eyes of the monster.

But the Chimera was so mad and wild with pain, that it did not guard itself well. In its efforts to stick its horrible iron claws into its enemy, the creature left its own breast exposed; and perceiving this, Bellerophon thrust his sword up to the hilt into its cruel heart. Immediately the snaky tail untied its knot. The monster let go its hold of Pegasus, and fell from that vast height, downward. The fire within its bosom, instead of being put out, burned fiercer than ever, and quickly began to consume the dead carcass.

Thus it fell out of the sky, all aflame, and (it being nightfall before it reached the earth) was mistaken for a shooting star or a comet. But, at early sunrise, some cottagers were going to their day's labor, and saw, to their astonishment, that several acres of ground were strewn with black ashes. In the middle of a field there was a heap of whitened bones a great deal higher than a haystack. Nothing else was ever seen of the dreadful Chimera!

And when Bellerophon had won the victory, he bent forward and kissed Pegasus, while the tears stood in his eyes.

HART

PUBLISHING

COMPANY